LIGHT IDEAS

BELIEVE IN GOD

DEREK RODGERS

KWE PUBLISHING

Rodgers, Derek. *Light Ideas: Believe in God*
Copyright © 2024 by Derek Rodgers all rights reserved.
ISBNs: 979-8-9913357-2-0 (paperback), 979-8-9913357-3-7, (ebook)

First Edition. All rights reserved. No portion of this book may be reproduced, stored in a retrieval system, or transmitted in any form or by any means - including but not limited to electronic, mechanical, digital, photocopy, recording, scanning, blogging or other - except for brief quotations in critical reviews, blogs, or articles, without the prior written permission of the publisher, KWE Publishing.

1
DO YOU BELIEVE IN GOD?

Do you believe in God? I don't need to believe, I know. This is a profession I made at different moments in my own life. I knew God was real. My instincts knew there was a force or an entity that existed outside of my own five senses. My mind, my heart, and my soul knew there was an entity or a creative force that organized life and the environment in which we live. I recently learned that a very well-known psychologist named Carl Jung voiced the same sentiment in an interview many years ago. He said, "I don't need to believe. I know."

Belief in God can be a simple idea or concept. Belief in God can also become a complex idea to understand and especially to live out. I believe in God. How do you know?

What exactly is belief? The meaning of belief must be defined. Is belief a statement? Is belief an action? Or is belief a spiritual

ritual practiced in the physical? Can a person prove his or her belief?

The second element is God. God must be defined to determine if I truly believe in God. What is God? Who is God? If there is a God, how do I validate my belief? Is it possible to believe in something that cannot be identified with the five senses? If there is a God, does that God believe in me? Believing in God can be a simple or a complex idea. I remember a time I claimed to believe, but I really didn't.

What is the definition of belief? There are several different definitions of belief. One definition is an acceptance that a statement is true or that something exists. A second definition is something one accepts as true or real. A third definition of belief is a firmly held opinion or religious conviction. Each definition expresses that belief is the affirming of a statement, idea, or concept.

What is the definition of God? There are many different definitions of God. I will reference a few of them. God, according to Christianity and other monotheistic religions, is the creator and ruler of the universe and source of all moral authority. God is the supreme being. In certain other religions, God is a superhuman being or spirit worshiped as having power over nature or human fortunes. God is the ultimate deity. Another use of the word "God" is an adored, admired, or influential person. This definition allows the user to refer to any exalted person or thing as a God.

Do you believe in God? Almost every human being does believe in a God. Every human exalts something or someone over themselves, even if it is just the possession of money. People do worship money. Everyone has a God. We all follow something or someone. We all worship something or someone. I believe there is a program embedded in the human soul. This program compels us all to obey a higher power. God also gave us the free will to choose who that higher power will be. Ask yourself. Do I believe in a God? If yes, who is your God? What is your God? Your life choices reveal who your God is.

The decisions you make each day are the proof of what you truly believe. I advise everyone I know to take some time to evaluate his or her life. Evaluate your current condition. Identify the source of inspiration that led you to do the things you do. I have done this several times. When my life is good, I do some self-evaluation. When my life is bad, I do some self-evaluation. My belief system leads to my daily choices. When my life was good, I was influenced by positive inspirations. When my life was bad, I was being influenced by negative inspirations. But I still claimed to believe in God.

The purpose of this small book is to help determine whether or not you and I truly believe in God and if that God we claim to believe in is Jesus Christ. When I was a child, I claimed to be a follower of Jesus Christ. I was honoring the traditions of my family and culture. It was the easy thing to do. I eventually did develop my own belief in God because of a few miraculous events. I had no trouble believing in God; I had trouble with the assimilation of religion and church.

People can sometimes deter a person's faith away from God. The actions of another person can remove a belief in God. We all must know God in a personal manner. Your belief and knowledge of God will continue regardless of the actions of other people. I always remember believing in God. But I despised the church and religion for many years. I had many debates with myself. If I believe in God, why do I allow people to change my mind and heart? And why do people who claim to believe in God hurt me?

This book was inspired by an interview I watched online. Dr. Jordan Peterson made some statements about faith that compelled me to organize my ideas about what a life with Jesus looks like. I had similar conversations with friends and family. But this particular interview compelled me to do more thinking. I also wanted to help people rediscover their purpose in life and know what that purpose does for the Kingdom of God. The God I know today is Jesus Christ.

After years of searching for truth, I now know there is a God. I now know that God has a name. His name is Jesus Christ. When I claim to believe in God, that claim comes with responsibility. I began to learn to obey the Bible and see what my belief in God would produce. Everything changed. The search for truth turned into a great adventure.

Every religion and faith will have a different impact on your life. This book is about what happens when your faith is in Jesus Christ. I will highlight my experiences and what the Bible states. Believing and following Jesus comes with a price. When a person states that he or she believes Jesus is God, a new life begins.

The world is looking for a light. People want to believe in something or someone. The people who lack faith in God want to see how the ones who do believe in God live. Just saying you believe is not enough. What does it look like to believe? People want to see evidence that God is real. People want to know how God takes care of His people. The world is looking for light because the landscape is dark. Men and women want a transcendent relationship that will enable them to escape their daily trauma and pain. If you believe in God, can we see it in your daily life?

I want to provide a simple outline of what it may look like to believe in God. It is more than just saying the words. Living for God is more than an affirmation. Believing in God entails a complete surrender to the God you claim to worship. If you believe, you will prove it with your actions. If you truly believe, your actions and behavior will proclaim your beliefs. This is what it means to be a disciple.

This book will highlight some of the elements that exemplify a true belief in God. Each element presents the physical, mental, and spiritual effort required to live a life of worship. Worship is the act or lifestyle of practicing your true beliefs. Once again, claiming to believe in God is much more than a mere mouthing of an affirmation. The actions and habits must prove the words we speak. The Bible states that God is a Spirit. And humans must worship and obey the Spirit through our spiritual adherence to God's law and live a life of truth.

This book will focus on Christianity. I am a follower of Jesus Christ. I can share my experiences and some of the information I gathered through Bible study. I can speak on how the walk of faith in Jesus requires courage and commitment, and it's forever. The person who truly believes Jesus is God understands it is a vow that lasts a lifetime.

Each element is a moment all the followers of Jesus Christ will endure. If you say you believe, these experiences will prove it. These experiences will test your devotion. These moments in your life will determine if you are who you say you are. At the end of your life, the goal is not just to believe in God; at the end of your life, you want to know God.

These are the events every believer in Jesus will endure. These are not in any particular order. Every person will have a different path in life. One element is the carrying of your cross. Another element the believer will experience is episodes of betrayal and abandonment. Most of us will also be faced with a painful, unjust death. Another form of suffering I endured, along with many others, is the deceitfulness of the masses. Each one of these sounds uncomfortable. And they are uncomfortable. But God uses all of these realities to make us perfect in His eyes.

2
CARRY YOUR CROSS

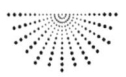

MARK 8:34

Jesus instructed all of the followers to deny their own plans and ideas for their lives and follow Jesus. This is usually one of the early tests of faith. The idea of carrying your own cross is not pretty. Denying oneself of pleasure and selfish pursuits is the opposite of what we are taught by society. Refusing to live for yourself is not the normal way of living. Almost all of our American life we are taught to live for ourselves.

One of the first messages I remember learning as a child was the idea that I can do what I want to do. Another idea I was taught early in life is that I can get whatever I want. Imagine the challenge of altering your attitude toward life as an adult. It is a real struggle to begin to think the way Jesus Christ wants you to think after learning the wrong way of thinking for your entire life. If I have been serving myself for my entire life,

I don't want to serve God. It feels like neglect. It feels strange.

The idea of carrying the cross involves executing your own ego. Carrying the cross involves putting the needs of others ahead of my own. Carrying the cross represents submitting to God's plan for my life. I must surrender my own plan for my own life. I am expected to make all of the same sacrifices Jesus Christ made. This process of surrender will challenge my belief system. The ones who claim to believe in God will completely surrender their lives to God. With the ultimate hope of a resurrection when the time is right.

I usually have trouble with the cross. There were times I felt God leading me to turn right but I wanted to turn left. There were other times I did turn right when I felt God prompting me to turn right. But I have to admit, this is one of the hardest tests. It is hard because we have a choice. This test of faith engages your free will. You don't have to do what God wants you to do.

If God says, take the job at the school. You don't have to do it. You can take the higher paying job that is less work. You may want to work as a truck driver. More money and less stress. But God may want you at the school to be a mentor and a good role model for the children. This is an example of the cross. Making tough choices. This is a simple employment example. There are other examples that require a deeper sacrifice.

Living a lifestyle of abstinence and

celibacy is a form of carrying the cross. It is a very hard challenge to abstain from physical pleasure. Most of our society is based on sex and physical pleasure. The need for sex is implanted into our minds at a very early age. I became obsessed with the desire for sex in high school.

Living for God requires men and women to avoid sex. The goal is to focus all of our mental, spiritual, and emotional strength on serving God. The Bible instructs men and women to avoid sex until they are married to another person who is serving God. The purpose is to build a family that will serve God and be an improvement to society. This happens by denying oneself immediate gratification. Most of us don't want to deny ourselves of sex. But this is mandatory for those who claim to believe.

A deeper example of carrying a cross would be serving as a missionary. I heard the testimony of a millionaire's son who joined a group of missionaries. He had the option to work for his father. This man could have lived a comfortable life. His father owned several businesses. This man could have made good money working for his family and chose not to suffer living in a foreign country. He chose to serve God.

There will be a moment in the life of every follower of Jesus Christ when he or she will be forced to make a choice. The choice is to surrender control of your life or continue doing what you planned to do with your own life.

3
BETRAYAL AND ABANDONMENT

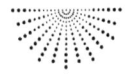

MATTHEW 5:11

Betrayal and abandonment are events that will happen to those who believe in God. The Bible reminds us all that Jesus was betrayed by those who walked close to Him. The Bible also reminds us of the moments when Jesus Christ was abandoned. Our faith and willpower must be proven if we claim to know God. The only way to know if you are a true believer is to endure the same way Jesus did.

I endured betrayal and abandonment many different times in my life. I failed to endure these painful moments with the same grace Jesus did. When I was betrayed, I became extremely angry and bitter. I failed to understand that these moments were lessons ordained by my Heavenly Father. I failed to realize how God was identifying my idols. On other occasions, the abandonment and betrayal were God attempting to rescue me from my enemies. Sometimes, we call our enemies friends.

Betrayal is very painful. Betrayal can only happen if it is committed by a person you once called friend or family. Betrayal cannot come from an enemy. The enemy was never trusted. Betrayal can only happen if trust is violated. The pain is the result of violated trust. No one wants to experience this pain. Betrayal is painful on many levels. Betrayal affects the nervous system and the psyche. I can probably write an entire book on the impact of betrayal.

Unfortunately, there are times when God allows betrayal. It must be done. The betrayal is for our protection. Men, women, and children have a tendency to place their trust in the wrong people and instead place their trust in other people who have status and power. These people become our authorities. It may seem harmless to follow other people, but the problems arise when we begin to obey people instead of God.

I remember some of the occasions when a spiritual leader I worshipped betrayed me. I remember how much it hurt to be mistreated by someone I honored. These moments forced me to go back to God. God is who I should have been worshipping, not another human. These spiritual leaders showed me their character flaws. I had to forgive them.

These abusive spiritual leaders are human, just like me. They will make mistakes just like anyone else. Sometimes they must be exposed. The exposure is not to humiliate them. The exposure is to free them from the impossible expectation of being perfect. We are only supposed to worship God, not other men and women.

Your faith in God will be tested when a family member betrays you. Can you forgive that person? Can you endure long-suffering? Betrayal from a family member is extremely painful. The worst part is that there is nowhere to go to avoid this person. It is almost impossible to erase family. It is easy to discard a friend or a coworker. But where do you go when a blood-born family member betrays you?

The test of faith in this scenario is forgiveness and long-suffering. God wants you to know if you can learn to love a person who hurt you. In order to learn the love of Jesus Christ, we must be taught to love our enemies. Sometimes, I think God allows certain people to hurt you. It is intentional. The goal is for you to endure long-suffering and control your temper. Forgiveness is easy to talk about. Forgiveness is a popular topic in church and in music. But actually doing it requires action.

I thought I knew what forgiveness was until I had to forgive someone from an incident in the past. I didn't know how much anger and bitterness was inside of me. I hid it well. I would actually lie and pretend I was not in pain. The bitterness I harbored was hindering my growth.

God allowed certain circumstances to unfold that forced me to deal with my unforgiveness. I had to address the past betrayal. This situation was extremely painful. I was physically exhausted as I dealt with my bitterness. Each one of us must learn to handle betrayal the correct way. God wants all believers to be spiritually strong and spiritually mature.

Abandonment is another painful experience most believers will endure. People who claim to love you will disappear from your life. Sometimes, friends and family will claim to be supportive, but they never show up when you need them. The absence of a support system produces extra stress and anxiety, especially if you were expecting to have help.

When I committed my life to God, I was abandoned by many people. A few of my friends did not understand how my life could experience a complete change. A few family members noticed my attitude change and they did not want to talk to me. When the abandonment happened, I was in shock. I was expecting everyone to follow Jesus after seeing me do it. I assumed my positive energy would be attractive. But that is not the reality. Some people are not attracted to God.

Those of us who truly believe in God must understand that everyone is not prepared to walk in the light. The presence of God will separate the people of light and the people of darkness. As much as I wanted everyone to be happy and born again, life don't work that way. Each man and each woman must go through the cross and encounter Jesus themselves. That is the only way.

Dealing with abandonment is a part of the process of becoming like Christ. The loss of friends and the loss of family will increase your dependence on God. The loss of friends and family will prevent you from placing your identity in other people. Losing people also teaches us that we really don't need them. We want them, but we don't need them. We need God. We need the guidance of the Holy Spirit.

The other lesson learned from abandonment is forgiveness. We must forgive the people who turn their backs on us. We must pray for the people who don't want to follow Jesus Christ with us. We must be patient and trust God to turn their hearts back to Him. The people who abandon you for following Jesus will return when it is their time to search for truth. Pray and forgive.

Each one of these tests and trials is designed to teach the follower how to trust God in everything. I am still learning.

4
PAINFUL UNJUST DEATH

1 PETER 2:19

Every follower of Jesus Christ will have moments of extreme persecution. It will be an unjust persecution. There are people who will hate you because of your faith. There are people who will attack you because of your obedience to Jesus Christ. The people who believe in God will receive hate and malice. This hate and malice will come from friends, family, coworkers, and maybe even strangers.

The malice that is directed toward you is not the same as the betrayal and the abandonment. This form of oppression is a direct attack against your character and your image. Betrayal and abandonment are deceptive tactics that will hurt you through absence and a lack of support. You feel pain through isolation and a lack of expected resources. But malevolence is a direct attack. It causes extreme pain. And malevolence will leave you exhausted.

The distress caused by malevolent behavior is overwhelming because you did not deserve it. The malice directed toward you is not warranted. When my name was defamed in public, I became angry and bitter. I wanted to retaliate. I wanted to enact revenge against the people who were spreading rumors about me. I wanted to hurt the people who hurt me. But this is what they wanted. The goal of these character attacks is to produce an evil response. These evil people want to prove that your faith is not real.

At times, the persecution will produce a death. This death is not always a physical death. The death produced by this form of malice is a character assassination. Your name will be defamed. Evil people who do not believe in God will seek to destroy your credibility. I endured a character assassination several times. It feels just like an unjust death. It's almost like the men who go to prison for a crime they did not commit. It's a mental torture.

Believing in God requires a submission to these character assassinations. It is an opportunity to prove how powerful our God really is. The malicious ones who choose to come against you, are doing it to hurt and harm you. They are doing it to tear down your faith. Their desired outcome is to prove that you and your God are not all-powerful. If they can destroy your name and your faith, it will justify their lack of faith. They don't want your God to be real.

The irony is that their attack will actually

make you and your faith become more evident. The attack forces you to pray and allow God to show His might. The character attacks will compel you to become a better person. The part of the attack that benefits you and God is now all eyes are on you. It is your opportunity to prove God is real to everyone witnessing the attack.

If the assassination attempt happened at your job, all of your coworkers are watching. If this attack happens at your church, all of the other church members are watching you. If this attack happens online, there will be an online audience waiting to see what happens. All of the attention is on the victim of the attack. This is another chance for God to perform a miracle.

The believer must maintain his or her integrity and practice self-control. This season of unjust death will become an awesome testimony later. When all eyes are on you during this attack, God will show how much power and glory is within you. This attack will draw nonbelievers to God.

People who never knew Jesus before this event will become curious and desire to search for truth. The attack will become your victory. I have seen this in my own life. I remember former coworkers who came to me in private with spiritual questions. I remember old friends who wanted to know more about Jesus after witnessing me overcome malice and unjust treatment. I maintained my integrity, and I did not seek revenge. The Lord Jesus Christ settled the affair. When Jesus settles a controversy, everyone will witness the results. And no one can deny who did it.

The Bible instructs us, "Be still, and know that I am God."

5
PERSECUTED BY THE MASSES

MATTHEW 5:11

There will be times when a true believer will be hated by the masses. There will be times when a believer will feel completely alone. The persecution we endure as believers is inevitable. The people who are living in opposition to God will become oppressive toward the people who live in accordance with God. Humans cannot remove God from His throne. All of their hatred and enmity against God will be redirected toward toward the people who worship Him. Unfortunately, the majority of humans do not follow the One True God. The real Christians are a minority on Earth. The majority of people live in a committed rebellion against God. And they will persecute the real followers.

I can remember how I was bullied in school for living as a professing Christian. The bullying was vicious and premeditated. I did not fully understand why I was mistreated. I was a young boy who thought people would like me because I was kind to them. But that is not what happened. I was verbally abused and physically abused by the students I showed love to. I learned a valuable lesson early in life. The people who are selfish and evil will take advantage of the people who are nice and kind. There is no fear of retaliation. Most Christians will not retaliate.

Those times I was enduring persecution from the masses, I realized most religious people are afraid to stand up and defend themselves. This was very confusing. I did not understand why Christian men and Christian women didn't fight back. I was very conflicted and very upset at the way we embarrassed the One True God. I never saw other students being attacked. I only witnessed myself and other Christian students endure the bullying. I wanted to fight back. Sometimes, I did fight back. But my heart was very disturbed.

I did not fully understand the purpose and the lessons God was teaching me through these events. I also did not realize there was a failure in the culture. Young saints are supposed to be disciplined in their walk with God at an early age. The older men should be shepherding the young men. I was never supposed to endure all of the abuse alone. This walk with God is a very hard walk. It is supposed to be hard. The more opposition you experience, the stronger you will become. God is a good father. HE is fully aware of our pain and our adversaries.

I have never met a mature and powerful Christian who did not endure persecution from the masses at some point in his or her life. The places the persecution comes from can vary. It may be at a school. The masses may form against you in the workplace. I can remember a time in the past when my coworkers would mistreat me. It was harsh and subtle. It was subtle because I didn't see it. Actually, I didn't want to see it. They knew what they were doing. I pretended not to notice because I was not prepared to confront them. It is hard to battle when you feel alone.

The schools we attend can become places where we are tortured. The workplace can become a spiritual battleground. But the worst place to receive hate from the masses is inside of a church. This is the worst location because it is supposed to be the place where we receive our edification. We go to church and expect to be safe. It is the one place, other than home, that a man, woman, or child should be able to let his or her guard down. We want to be vulnerable. We want to expose ourselves to others with the expectation of receiving healing.

True believers will be challenged and persecuted inside of a church. I have seen it and witnessed it myself. It is a form of malevolence that cannot be comprehended because it does not make any sense. It was especially confusing to me as a child. I was naïve and chose to love people. I expected the love to be returned. I assumed everyone in the church was a saint. I assumed everyone in the church wanted to be good. I was wrong.

I can write many stories about how I was singled out in church. I can recall many occasions of abuse I experienced inside of a church. One of the worst persecutions I endured from the masses was when I decided to remain celibate. Many of the other teenagers in the church were not celibate. A few of them became parents as teenagers. I decided to obey God and remain a virgin. I was viciously attacked for that. A few people spread a rumor that I was gay. This was humiliating. I had my name and reputation slandered because I chose to be obedient to the Bible.

This church attack was very traumatizing to me because I felt like no one defended me. I expected the elders and the authority figures to defend me and my honor. But that did not happen. I saw the elders and the ministry leaders protect, defend, and support the teenagers who were having children outside of wedlock. Why would church leaders cover for the teenagers who were doing wrong and not support or defend the teenagers who chose to do the right thing? Sometimes, the masses are completely wrong.

Church hurt is a real phenomenon. It may seem unbelievable. But it is a fact. It may even scare some people away from the faith. If you are not safe inside of a church, where are you safe?

The true believers must understand and be prepared for spiritual warfare. This warfare will come from any and everywhere. The masses who isolate you and then attack you can be friends, family, or coworkers. There is one encouraging sign during this difficult trial. Whenever the masses rally against you, it is evidence you are on the right side.

AFTERWORD

I experienced every one of these elements during my walk with God. Each one of these created a desire in my heart to know who God is even more. I was compelled to intensify my search for truth. The persecution and the pain forced me to identify my weakness and my true identity. God is a good Father. God allows these stressful events. These stressful events are designed to remove the trash from our lives. These stressful events are designed to uncover false belief systems. These events are used to make us holy and perfect. The ones who truly believe will endure these tests and trials. The ones who truly believe will not change their minds. The ones who truly believe will become like Christ.

What you behold is what you become.

ABOUT THE AUTHOR

The author, Derek Rodgers, is a writer and podcaster originally from Newport News, Virginia. He is a husband and father of three children. Derek has experience teaching and preaching in correctional institutions and churches. He has also coached youth sports and does volunteer work in the community. He hopes to inspire other men and women to seek God in everything they do. The author has birthed a nonprofit organization in Richmond, Virginia, that will provide mentoring and life coaching to teenagers in search of identity and direction.

You can email Derek at drodgers@dofourtreach.com and find him at @Theillegitimatepodcast on Instagram, @Theillegitimatepodcast on TikTok, and The Illegitimate Game on Youtube.

Milton Keynes UK
Ingram Content Group UK Ltd.
UKHW021912281024
450365UK00017B/741

GODFATHER OF THE GALAXY

By:
Mark Castleberry

Copyright ©2024 Mark Castleberry

All rights reserved. No part of this publication may be reproduced, distributed, or transmitted in any form or by any means, including photocopying, recording, or other electronic or mechanical methods, without the prior written permission of the publisher, except in the case of brief quotations embodied in critical reviews and certain other noncommercial uses permitted by copyright law. For permission requests, write to the publisher, addressed "Attention: Permissions Coordinator," at the web address below.

ISBN: 979-8-3302-0232-4 (Paperback)
ISBN: 979-8-3302-0231-7 (e-Book)

Library of Congress Control Number: 2024921250

SECOND EDITION
Any references to historical events, real people, or real places are used fictitiously. Names, characters, and places are products of the author's imagination.

Permission to use material from other works
Conflict With Shadows (2019, 2013) and Into Shadow's Fire (2022, 2023)
Godfather Of The Galaxy (Amazon Edition 2020)
By Mark Castleberry

Front cover image by Wonder.
Edited By: Becky Schulz

Printed in United States of America

Published by Strangers and Pilgrims Publishing
 www.strangerspilgrims.com

Dedicated to my family
for being there throughout all my bad
decisions.

And of course this is for my wife,
who was one of my best decisions,
and who put up with me during the ups
and downs of my writing,

And, behold, one came and said unto him, Good Master, what good thing shall I do, that I may have eternal life? And he said unto him, Why callest thou me good? there is none good but one, that is, God: but if thou wilt enter into life, keep the commandments. He saith unto him, Which? Jesus said, Thou shalt do no murder, Thou shalt not commit adultery, Thou shalt not steal, Thou shalt not bear false witness, Honour thy father and thy mother: and, Thou shalt love thy neighbour as thyself.

The young man saith unto him, All these things have I kept from my youth up: what lack I yet? Jesus said unto him, If thou wilt be perfect, go and sell that thou hast, and give to the poor, and thou shalt have treasure in heaven: and come and follow me.

But when the young man heard that saying, he went away sorrowful: for he had great possessions.

- Matthew 19:16-24 KIV

TABLE OF CONTENTS

Mobsters....................8

First Job...................17

Off-World................26

The Loyalty Crew.......37

Chimera....................47

Family And War..........63

Time To Settle............73

The Godfather...........81

The Deal...................89

Two Years Later.........99

Jonah......................106

CHAPTER ONE
MOBSTERS

Thermonte stood in one of the upper rooms of his father's business, looking down into the street from a large window, looking below, watching the action taking place. It was on the other side of the street; two men dressed in black overcoats, confronting the store owner from across the street. One man stood behind the store owner, the other spoke to him in front of him.

The front man hit the shop owner in the stomach with his fist, and with his other hand, patting him on his shoulder. To

Thermonte, it reminded him of when his own father yelled at him when he had done something wrong. The finger pointing and shaking, and the business owner down on his knees in front now. The streets were empty this morning, probably because most everyone here in the District of Caste was getting ready to go to temple in a few hours.

"Thermonte, go get yourself dressed young man!" yelled his mother reminding him, as she passed his room.

He ignored her, still watching the men outside. Thermonte was a quiet boy. He had just turned eight years old, just two months ago. He had few friends, just those he knew from school, and he spent most of his time looking out of his window in his room. His mother was a strict woman and didn't want him playing out in the streets with the other kids, and she usually dragged him to the Caste Temple of Light every week, where he usually took brief naps during service.

In the days ahead, Thermonte would always see what happened next in slow motion. One man, standing in the back of the business owner outside, pulled out a *mark x*1, slender barreled blast pistol pointing the barrel at the back of the owner's head, and shot a hole in it.

Thermonte didn't even blink. It was just another killing in the streets. The Locals would arrive and do an investigation, and he and his mother would walk to the temple as they always had, and nothing would ever be done. It never was.

"Thermonte!" he heard his mother calling to him from her own bedroom, "It's time to get ready!"

They lived in the three-bedroom apartment just above the Deli his father owned. His father owned the building, as far as he was concerned. Thermonte turned his head with that last call, and he finally moved to get dressed to go out.

A few moments later, his mother stuck her head in his door. "Hurry yourself up!" she said.

"Mom," he said to her, "Is dad not going?"

"He has business this morning," she replied. "Now hurry. We got to get going."

About thirty minutes later, Thermonte walked down the stairs into the Deli where he saw his father sitting at one of the tables. He waved to him, and his father waved back. Holding his mother's hand, he followed her out of the door of the Deli, and began the walk to the temple.

As he walked, Thermonte turned his head around to see a long black air-car pulled up next to his father's Deli, and saw who was getting out. It was the head of the Corlesh Clan, the biggest mob family on the planet of Chotis. Jerking his hand, his mother warned him not to watch, and they turned the corner and the Deli disappeared from sight.

On the world of Chotis, in the city of Strauss, in the District of Caste, was The Electrik Deli. The owner was Thorn Electrik. It had been standing there for almost ten years and was still standing when Thermonte and his mother returned from services. He followed her into the store entrance and she locked it behind them. They both headed up the stairs to go home.

He saw his father sitting at the kitchen table looking over some paperwork. That really didn't worry Thermonte, because he had other things on his mind.

His mother escorted him into his room. "Get out of your church clothes and put on some play ones. We'll eat some lunch soon."

"Yes, ma'am." he answered, being polite as they had always tried to teach him. He closed his door, but he could still hear what was being said in the kitchen, as his mother prepared his lunch.

"What did they want?" she asked him.

"It's the same laundering scam," replied his father. "And they want to use the store, a few nights from now. They'll send a guy around to get the key."

"I don't like it."

"Neither do I, but I didn't make the payment this month, so it's this or you lose a husband."

There was a moment of silence, where Thermonte could hear nothing.. Then his mom said, "I hate this place. Let's move out of Stromberg, maybe even Chotis."

"We don't have the money to move. I make a good living here. We all have food in our mouths, a roof over our heads, and Thermonte is even going to a good school. Maybe we can't leave here, but perhaps he will."

"You're right." she replied. "But, I don't trust the Corlesh Clan."

"If we don't cross them, they will leave us alone." he said.

"Except for monthly payments, which takes nearly half of our income."

Things were silent after that, and all was well after. Thermonte went into the kitchen and sat opposite his father. His mother put down sandwiches for lunch and Thermonte received a glass of milk.

His father had put up the paperwork and

was smiling at him. Then he smiled at his wife as she put the rest of the lunch on the table. "Everything should be fine," he told her. "I promise."

They all sat down and ate lunch together.

Thermonte woke up. It was dark outside, except for the blue lights flashing outside all around. He could hear movement downstairs in the Deli and even up here in the apartment. Somewhere in the house, he heard his mother crying.

Thermonte slid out of his bed onto his bare feet and walked over to the window. Locals were everywhere. He watched as a pair of paramedics carried out a body from his father's store and then brought out others. He didn't know what was going on.

He tiptoed to his bedroom door and cracked it. His mother was obviously on the other side of the apartment, by the crying he heard, but he caught the voices of several of the inspectors.

"Where did you find him?" asked one man.

Thermonte knew about Locals, and he knew this man was in charge. He had seen him before.

"In the back." replied the other man. "Looks like they tortured him. Arm in the grinder, and then shot twice. Once in the thigh, and once in the head."

"Deli owner?"

"Yep. His wife said it was the Corlesh Clan. They had come back the other day to set up an appointment to use the Deli, and Mr. Electrik agreed. When they came here for their appointment, they asked him to come down. And then they killed him."

The man in charge thought for a moment. "You know it will be hard to get a conviction on this. The Corlesh have control of a lot of different things in the city. They own this city."

"What about her?" the inspector asked. "They may come back for her."

"We'll keep our eyes out. Best we can do. The Corlesh Clan won't hurt women and children. I will make sure of that."

After they had walked off, back down to the Deli, Thermonte realized that they would do nothing. He hated the Corlesh Clan for killing his father, and he hated the Locals for not doing anything about it. Even at eight, he would do whatever he had to do to get his revenge. He would get his revenge on his father with the Corlesh Clan. He would also get revenge for his mother by dealing with the Locals.

He opened his door and drifted toward his mother's room where she was crying. The Locals were gone from the upstairs, at least for the moment, and Thermonte just crawled up next to her and hugged her. She embraced him and continued to cry for the rest of the night.

CHAPTER TWO
FIRST JOB

He had just gotten off from school and was making his way with one of his friends. He was fourteen, as was his friend, and they had been best friends for three years now. His friend's name was Derik Poe. After moving from above the deli five years ago, Thermonte's mom moved them halfway across the planet to the Cinder District in the city of Necros. It was also a poor district in another city, but his mother was trying to get him away from the criminal element there.

Thermonte knew, however, it was the

Corlesh Clan she was getting away from after they had pushed her to pay protection money. She then just sold the deli, and they had moved. Now to make money, she had become a cleaning lady for local businesses in the area.

Thermonte and Derik were walking home from school, their mothers worked together; which is the reason the boys would walk together, and had become such good friends. They both lived in small apartments about five blocks from the school. It was the same building, same floor, and their apartments were nearly across the hall from one another. That started them being best friends five years back.

"Hey kid." He heard a voice. It was coming from a nearby building, where a set of brick stairs led down several feet to the basement of the building. It was cold, so the man wore a cap on his head with only a ponytail of hair being revealed down his back.

Thermonte stopped and looked. "Me?" he

asked, pointing to himself.

The man nodded. "Yea you." He said. "You want to make some money?"

Thermonte thought that was a stupid question. Of course he wanted to make some money. He and his mom could use a little extra. "What do I have to do?"

Derik whispered in his friend's ear. "We gotta get home."

"Our moms will never know." he whispered back.

The man in the cap pulled out a bulky envelope out from under his coat and handed it to him. "Do you know where Strutter Street is?"

Thermonte nodded that he did. And he did. It was back in the opposite direction.

The man continued, "Go to 364 South Strutter Street, knock on the door and ask for a man called Shade."

Thermonte nodded. He understood everything. "Okay." he said.

"Give this package to him. Tell him

Khanel sent you. He will pay you. If he doesn't come see me down here."

Thermonte nodded again and left. The man, calling himself Khanel, made his way back into the basement door.

As Derik followed his friend, he stopped him. "I think those are bad guys." he said, not knowing how to describe them. He wasn't sure who they were, but he had seen things around the neighborhood.

"If you don't want to go, then go wait for me at our building. Our moms won't be home for several hours. If I can help my mom make some extra money to help her, I will."

Derik walked a block with him, but then chickened out. He told Thermonte he would meet him back home and ran off in the opposite direction. Thermonte just continued on his way to do his job.

It took him almost twenty minutes to reach the storefront on Strutter Street. It was a jewelry shop of a sort, called Strange Gems, and it looked like it catered to the older kids.

The door was locked, and so Thermonte rang the bell that was provided.

A man came to the door, dressed in a fine business suit of black and silver. "Yes?" He looked down and saw the fourteen-year-old looking back up at him. "And how may I help such a young one?"

The man was tall and slender. He looked like a giant from young Thermonte's eyes. It took a moment for him to speak. "Um, Khanel sent me."

"Who you here to see?"

"Someone called Shade."

The man opened the door wider and ushered Thermonte inside. "Follow me." he said after closing the door, and made his way across the store and into the back, then down a hallway. The man knocked on the door on the end.

"Yea!" came a muffled shout from behind the door.

The man smiled at Thermonte. Then to the voice, he said, "Khanel sent a boy to see you."

After a very short pause, the man told him to send him in. Thermonte walked in, still holding the package. "Are you Shade, sir?"

The man behind the desk looked up at the tall man and smiled. "Yea kid, I'm Shade."

Shade had a good tan from the sun, and short black hair sticking up a little from the top of his head. There was a small tattoo on his chin, or was that hair? Thermonte couldn't tell. He handed the package to Shade, and said, "Khanel told me you would pay me for this."

Shade waved for him to hand him the envelope, and Thermonte handed it to him. He knew the other guy would pay him if this one did not. Shade opened the package and took a peek inside. Then he looked at the slender man and nodded at him.

The slender man walked over to a small opened safe, grabbed something and walked over to stand beside Thermonte, handing him something. The boy took it. It was fifty talents in coin. He had gotten paid, and very well too. Thermonte knew his mom only made about two hundred talents in a week cleaning.

Shade smiled at the boy. "You can go now, son. Now go home."

With that, the slender man led him back across the jewelery store and out the door. With the money in his pocket, he walked home and found his friend waiting on the front stoop.

It was two days later, Thermonte and his friend were walking home from school again, when Khanel called to him again. Unafraid, Thermonte walked on over, followed by his cautious friend.

"You did well the other day." the man said. "How would you like a permanent job, working for me?"

Thermonte could feel his friends' eyes on him, but he didn't pay attention. "What would I have to do?" he asked him.

"You know this neighborhood good, don't

you?" the man asked, and Thermonte nodded. Khanel continued. "You would deliver packages for me. I will pay for every delivery you do. One hundred talents per delivery."

That would help his mom, he thought. Maybe she wouldn't have to work so much. Looking at the man he asked, "Would I be working every day?"

"You can stop by after school, but the deliveries only take place every other day, sometimes every day, sometimes not."

Thermonte thought back about when he had come home the other day, that Derik had realized how much money he had made, and wanted to do some deliveries. So with that in mind, he asked about that. "Can my friend get a job too?"

Khanel looked around him and at Derik. Derik was smaller than Thermonte. Then he said, "He works for you, and you pay him out of your payment. He messes up, you take care of him. Fair?"

Thermonte looked back at his friend, who

was staring back at him, nervous and waiting. He looked back at Khanel. "That's fair."

"Good." the man said. "Come by tomorrow. I'll have something for you then."

With that, Thermonte and Derik began their jobs. They walked home, and vowed not to tell their mothers about this, but keep the money hidden until they had enough to really take their mothers away from this life.

The next day, Thermonte and Derik made their first hundred. They split it, for they would do everything together. And that continued on for several years, and Thermonte considered this to be some of his better times.

CHAPTER THREE
OFF-WORLD

Thermonte Electrik sat across from his employer, a name named Khanel, whom he had been working for, for nearly four and a half years. Thermonte was soon to be a graduate from his primary school, and would move away from home.

"So tell me, how would you like to move up in this organization?" Khanel asked him. "After you graduate."

"My mom wants me to go to college." Was his reply. "I have gotten two offers to go off world to get a higher education."

"I can offer you a job that pays very well and has off world assignments."

"What kind of assignments?"

Khanel smiled. "Same as you do here," he replied. "Only these pay much more than local assignments."

Thermonte thought about it for a moment. I could make something out of this job. It was easy and paid very well. "Who will take care of the local ones?"

"I thought about your friend, Derik," said the boss. "He's been with you all this time, has he not? And so I think it would be good for him to go out alone. Everyone knows him."

Thermonte thought about Derik. He could do this minor job on his own, allowing himself to move up and take assignments off world. His friend had gotten better at working this job and had actually taken on drops when he was sick and couldn't make them. This had occurred several times. He had gotten very proud of Derik, and they worked well together.

To Khanel, he said, "I need to wait until after graduation. It's for my mom, you know."

"Oh, I understand. Your mother is protected as long as you are with us, you know that. Nothing will happen to her while you are on assignment. You guys have become family."

Thermonte nodded. "Okay," he said. "I'll do it. But I will need at least a week after graduation. I'll tell my mom I am checking out schools or something. She doesn't need to know what I do."

"She would be against it, huh?"

"My mom is a big churchgoer, and wants to see me more involved in God and everything, so I don't want her to know I am involved in this."

He had long known that he was doing illegal jobs with Khanel. Khanel had accepted this and never denied what he always did or gave excuses to Thermonte. He liked the young lad and was taking him under his wing to help him. Khanel's father would be proud.

The other boy Derik would have to be watched. And that is exactly what he had planned to do when Thermonte had moved up.

"It's a deal, Monte." Khanel told him. He had always called him Monte, and Thermonte had liked it. It meant they trusted him. He continued, "So in ninety-six days, I will have your first assignment ready."

Thermonte stood up to leave. "Sounds good." he said, and they shook hands in friendship. "I'll see you tomorrow." Then he left, and Khanel continued to take care of business.

He had finally graduated school, and as far as his mother knew, he was heading off-world to the world of Tiere for his higher education. Thermonte was leaving his world of Chotis, and he would get some higher education, but he was not heading to Tiere.

It was his last full day here with his mother, and he went to the temple with her.

She had always wanted him to invest his time into the temple and worshiping the Lord of Light, and into the things of the church. But that was not his thoughts. He saw that most leaders in the temple were not rich and did not have a lot of money. The job he had, had made him well off. And so, he had already decided to stay in the business.

So at the temple, they had a celebration for him going off to higher education on Tiere. Then he left and spent the rest of the day with his mother. He had to make all of the normal promises one makes to their mother when they go off for the first time. Some he knew would be easy to keep. Others, not so much.

The next morning, he had packed up his gear and said his goodbyes to his mother. He climbed into the air-cab that was waiting. The air-cab driver worked for Khanel and took him directly to his boss's office.

"Are you ready for your assignment?" Khanel smiled as he watched Thermonte walk in. He threw over an envelope across his desk.

Thermonte picked up the envelope and opened it, looking at the contents. "You are sending me to Ofidian Station?"

"Surprised?"

Thermonte knew what this meant. It reminded him of who had killed his father. The Corlesh Clan owned the Ofidian Station and ran the organization from there. "What am I going to do there?"

Khanel walked around the desk, patting him on the back. "Working for the crew. We have promoted you Monte." he said, and it was then Thermonte knew.

Thermonte Electrik had been working for the very people that had murdered his father those many years ago. He had been a part of the Corlesh Clan this whole time. Inside, he grew angry, and he wanted to strike back. But his persona kept cool, and he showed no urge on his outward appearance. Anyway, it wasn't Khanel he was needing to kill, it was those at the top. He wanted the godfather of the clan. From there, he could work down the ladder.

A plan formed in his mind that quickly, and he continued to think about it as he left and headed to the spaceport. There, a private ship waited for him. A yacht class freighter was there just for him, sent by the clan to take him to the station. He would need people with him to help. He already had one, but Derik was staying behind on Chotis. For the moment he would keep the thought in his head, where no one could find it.

Three days later, Thermonte Electrik stepped on the Ofidian Station for the first time. He had made it off-world, and it was time to start his new life.

The Ofidian Station was a mobile station. It moved around often, so that the Republic Agents wouldn't find it. It was also known as a pleasure station, or casino station where, if his mother might call it, a station of sin. There was everything that you did not want to follow you back to your home life. For everything here was private and everything stayed on the station. Just as long as you paid your bill or debts.

A man who called himself Jazy, who claimed to be the godfather's right hand, met him. He was actually more of a personal secretary. There was no need for guards, because they were scattered like a militia throughout the corridors of the station. All around him, drunken and partying people, were having what they considered to be a good time.

Jazy led him through several doors after riding on a lift heading to one of the top floors. All of this led closer to the center of the station, where he finally met Corlesh Clan godfather, San Corlesh.

"Welcome my boy." he said in a big haunting voice. He sat behind a large wooden desk and did not stand when Thermonte entered. He was an overly large man smoking a cigar and drinking a glass of some toxic drink. "My son has nothing but good things to say about you."

"Your son?"

"Khanel." the godfather smiled. "Khanel

Corlesh. You mean he didn't tell you?" To the others in the room, he said, "Doesn't that sound just like Khanel? He won't use his surname. And he is right." he said to Thermonte. "He finds more loyalty that way."

For the first time, Thermonte noticed the other two people in the room. Later he would find out they were associates of his, who had been there for other business.

"Mister Clought here needs a job done, and I think you could be the one here to do it, if you are ready like Khanel says." The godfather was referring to the red head man, half the size of himself. All three had drinks and were smoking cigars.

Thermonte thought for a moment. "What kind of job is it?"

"Does it matter?" San asked him, not expecting an answer. "You do this job; you do this job well, and you get your own crew."

"A crew?"

"Four or five others working under you. You pick your own team and you vouch for your team. Otherwise I come down on you," San Corlesh explained. "So you pick your crew and you make sure of their loyalty. If they betray you or this clan in some way, it will be up to you to handle the situation."

Thermonte stood there. He could use his own crew. A crew loyal to him and him alone.

Jokingly, the man the godfather referred to as Mister Clought, said, "Perhaps the boy thinks he is too young."

San looked over at him. "Khanel had his own crew at that age. He even worked the streets on Chotis a year later." He turned back to Thermonte. "Well, what do you say? Are you up for this job?"

Thermonte shifted his eyes to Mister Clought, then back to the godfather. "I'm in." he said.

San Corlesh smiled. "Good." he said. Then to Jazy, he said, "Get young mister Electrik settled in his apartment." Then to Thermonte he said, "Take a shower, relax, eat, and in the morning I will have the details ready for your job."

Thermonte nodded his agreement. "Yes, sir." Then he was led away.

CHAPTER FOUR
THE LOYALTY CREW

Thermonte Electrik sat on board a commercial spaceflight heading to the world of Tiere. Specifically, the capitol city of Sandal. It was here that his special delivery was to take place. If this succeeded, Thermonte would be well on his way.

The craft landed in the bay, and Thermonte made his way off the spacecraft and through the spaceport, finding an air cab quickly. They usually waited there, hoping to get an enormous tip. They had given Thermonte enough money to do just that.

"Alliance Senatorial Office, please." he said in his friendly tone.

The cab driver shrugged and really thought nothing about it since his rider was dressed like someone who worked there.

Thermonte carried a lightweight briefcase and wore a multi-layered suit much like a Senator would wear. He looked nice and clean. It took nearly an hour to reach the building. Once there, he climbed out of the cab, asked for him to wait, and headed inside the building.

He walked up to the front desk. "I'm here to see a Mister Pallinky." he told the desk clerk. Mister Pallinky worked for the Senator of Chotis, Senator Powell.

The clerk called a number, then spoke to Thermonte. "What is this pertaining too?"

Thermonte returned a friendly smile. "I have a delivery for him from one Mr. Clought."

According to what Thermonte had been told, this Pallinky was on the take and they used him to sway the votes of Senator

Powell. He didn't know what was in the briefcase, but he suspected it was cash and orders.

After speaking briefly to Pallinky, he spoke then to Thermonte. "He is on his way down." He indicated seating where he could wait. Thermonte nodded and thanked him and went to sit down.

A few moments later, Pallinky walked out and met Thermonte. Thermonte handed him the briefcase, and Pallinky leaned in and whispered in his ear. "Tell Clought, I'm done." Then he smiled and went back to where he had come from.

Thermonte just shrugged and walked out of the building and into his awaiting cab. "Back to the spaceport please." he told the driver; and that is where the driver took him. Several hours later, he was on board another commercial spaceflight heading back to Chotis. It was there he would pick his crew, which was promised him.

During this point, the Tiere News reported an explosion in the Senatorial building, killing ten people. One was the Chotis Senator, and another was the man Thermonte had handed the briefcase to, Pallinky. The other eight were office employees. Thermonte only learned about this after landing on Chotis. It made no impact on him, because he knew who he was now working for.

On Chotis, he met up with Khanel Corlesh, and together they helped Thermonte form his team.

While he was on Chotis, Thermonte did not go see his mother. She never knew he had been there during his recruiting mission.

The first person he grabbed on his team was his long-time friend, Derik Poe. Khanel had told him that Derik was doing good, and that he could hire any kid off the street; but, it was decided that Derik would continue to work for Khanel on Chotis while also working for his friend Thermonte. Since Derik's mother had already passed on several years back, Thermonte told Derik that his primary job was to watch his mother against the Clan. Derik agreed.

The next one he grabbed was strictly for the man's brawn and muscle. The man's name was Leon Gar. He used to be a bully back when Thermonte was young. But Leon had always liked him, because he had once gotten Leon out of some trouble. So Leon agreed to join.

The third man was a man named Ivan Stromberg. He was a known assassin who worked freelance for a time, but something had gone wrong. He had gotten captured by Republic Agents and had spent time in the Black Star prison; only to escape on a work furlough on the moon of Jasper many years ago. The Corlesh Clan had hidden him and given him a job working on the inside and changing his face. His face was now scarred and rough. But he was a good man, and this was a step up for him to work with this young man. Ivan knew all about loyalty. To him, being loyal to Thermonte, he would be loyal to the Clan.

After leaving Chotis, leaving Derik there, in a private transport class ship, he went to the world of Pandaris. On Pandaris, he and his crew met the newest members of his team. Two men who looked like they could work in the financial world. Designer suits, clean cut, no scars; but according to what Thermonte had heard and known of them, they were deadly. They were happy to give up their lives on Pandaris to work for a crew for the Corlesh Clan. The Corlesh Clan was the biggest syndicate in the galaxy.

The two men were friends and had run cons and such together before. Their names were Hester Boyd and Scotch Kammel. So four months after officially joining Thermonte's crew, they left the world of Pandaris, and headed out among the stars and home to the Ofidian Station. But when Thermonte had gotten to the last known coordinates, they found it missing.

Now Thermonte knew that the station would move from place to place, hiding from the law. He also knew that if the station was not there, the law was near. And sure enough, in the distance, sat a Republic

Alliance Battle Cruiser.

Thermonte was in the pilot seat, and he shouted back at the others. "Anyone have any open warrants on them that might cause problems?"

No one knew if they had or not. "Well, we are about to see." Thermonte told them. "Alliance Battle Cruiser is nearly on top of us."

Then there was the standard communication coming through. "This is the Republic Battleship Stoneguard. Send ID and registration number." This was a command.

Thermonte replied. "This is the personal transport class ship Hopper 7, sending registration now."

After a few moments, the Stoneguard was on top of them. Then the Republic ship communicated again. "Transport ship Hopper 7, what is your purpose for being here?"

Thermonte knew there would only be one reason they would be here, but he had to come up with something else. He knew the Republic would only be here looking for the Ofidian Station. After not being able to come up with something quickly, Thermonte heard another communication from the Republic.

"Hopper 7, be prepared to enter bay twelve, and to be boarded. Have the identification of all of your passengers ready."

Thermonte shouted back at the others. "Get ready, we're being boarded."

It took about ten minutes to dock in the bay and to hear a knock on the outer hull. Thermonte opened it and Republic soldiers marched in and led them all out during the search. Thermonte saw an officer heading toward them.

The officer's hair was dark brown, just starting to gray. His face clean shaven, and by his ways, Thermonte knew this man lived the corp. "I'm Captain Shepherd. Tell me what you were doing here in these coordinates."

A few seconds passed, then it was Scotch who spoke up. "I'm getting married, and we heard about a party station here."

"You mean the Ofidian Station?" Shepherd asked him.

"Yea," Scotch replied. "I was going to take some of my friends and go party for a week, before, you know, I get tied down."

Captain Shepherd moved closer to him and just looked him over for a moment. Then he said, "How did you hear about this station? Mister…"

"Kammel," Scotch finished the sentence. "And the station is legendary, man. Everyone knows about it. Getting to it is just the hard part."

The soldiers then came out of the transport and one of them, who was in charge, walked over to the Captain. "Found nothing, Captain." he said.

"Very well." Captain Shepherd said, looking at all four of the men. He stopped at Thermonte. "I have a feeling you will be trouble. So be careful of your actions."

Thermonte just smiled and nodded. "I will, sir." he said.

Captain Shepherd moved away and told his soldiers to release them, then told them to get out of this area. Once they had gotten back into space, and the Republic ship had moved away, Thermonte reset coordinates and headed back to Chotis.

Khanel Corlesh met them at the private spaceport where they needed to do a thorough scan of the ship, inside and out. They found nothing on the ship, nor inside the software. Khanel then gave them the updated coordinates to the Ofidian Station. They were off then, and two days later, they were comfortably eating dinner in one of the casinos on the station.

CHAPTER FIVE
CHIMERA

For three years, Thermonte's crew had been bringing in the money for the family and had been making money for themselves. Thermonte himself had put away much of the money he had made with the clan. The Corlesh Clan godfather called in Thermonte into his office, this time alone. The rest of his crew were to meet him later in one of the many casinos on board.

"You've done a fantastic job for me and the family." San Corlesh started the conversation. "I think it's time I give you and your crew a different mission, so to speak."

"A promotion, I suppose?" Thermonte replied, and he was smiling.

"Yea, in a way. You and your crew have a knack of getting out of trouble and away from the law, both local and those pesky Republic Agents. I want you and your crew out and about the galaxy and help me in our expanse. We are expanding, and soon we will be in the Federation. I need a crew like yours to get around the law and help bring more into the Clan."

Thermonte smiled. "Seems like you want to overthrow the governments and rule the galaxy yourself."

San was smiling, and he raised an eyebrow. "It's the dream, my friend."

Thermonte took a deep breath at the thought. It was enticing, but he knew San Corlesh could not handle it. But he was interested. "I will need my own personal ship, not those personal transports," he said.

San handed him a cash card. "Take this to the Ikon Shipyards, and design and purchase your crew a yacht class ship. That should be big enough to live in for months at a time. Talk to a friend of mine named Joe Sharp. He works in design, and will oversee any extra features you might want to put in."

"Reliable?"

"We've used him before." answered the godfather. "Tell him the Corlesh Clan appreciates his help."

Thermonte nodded and stood up. "I thank you." he said to him. Inside, he knew this was a step in the right direction for his own agenda.

The Ikon Shipyards were located on the far side of the three moons of Gin Kojoda, which expanded along the boarders of the Federation and the Republic. A sparse asteroid belt surrounded the star system on three sides. The world of Gin Kojodo was alone in the system but for its three moons which circled the planet one right after the other. That is what it looked like if you were standing on the surface. The system's sun was beyond the belt, and the light had to pass through it to shine on the world itself. That made daytime on Gin Kojoda almost grey.

That world is where the primary base for the shipyard was located, surrounded by a large electrical fence. Within that fence were the only living people on the planet.

Thermonte brought Leon with him for a bit of muscle. They had taken a smaller long distance shuttle craft, since it was to be a quick trip. He found Joe Sharp in his office, and it seemed he was talking to another man.

The other man was a very tall, slender man, dressed in a very fine suit. His hair was black and slicked back. It was short and seemed to not have anything out of place. He turned around when Joe looked up and saw them coming toward them. He had a big grin on his face, and his teeth looked as if they sparkled.

It was Joe who spoke up first. "You must be Thermonte Electrik." he said, and they walked toward them standing around a large table standing about waist high. "Mister Corlesh called ahead and told me to expect you."

"That's me." Thermonte said. He noticed that there were plans of a large ship on the table; almost as large as a battleship.

The tall man looked over to him and offered his hand. "My name is Doctor Phaleg." he said, and he wrapped his long fingers around Thermonte's hand. It made Thermonte almost feel weird.

"I'm supposed to design and have a ship built for him." Joe told the Doctor "A gift from his employer."

"Ahh,.." smiled Phaleg. "I know Mister Corlesh well. We are discussing a viable business proposition."

Thermonte grunted lightly. "I have heard nothing about it."

"No one has yet. It's only between us." Then to Joe, he said, "Perhaps I should go and let you two get to work. My ship can wait, let's get this man's ship built."

"As you say." Joe told him, and he and Thermonte watched him walk off. He seemed to be a properly rich man, odd; but when you are rich, you can afford to be odd.

Still, Thermonte would need to find out what this business he was talking about was. Now, however, he needed to get his ship built. It took nearly three days to design the craft. His design was that of a yacht class ship; the outer hull was of silver and trimmed in gold. If he was going to do his job, he would need to appear rich.

He was near to it. He had been saving his money, ready to use it for a rainy day.

So, on the fourth day, Thermonte and Leon took off from the Ikon Shipyards and headed back to the Ofidian Station. There, another mission was given to him and his team from the boss.

Serenity, the most peaceful world in the known galaxy. It hung in space between the borders, between the two major factions just outside their control. It was a world where everyone would visit in harmony regardless of their own personal political beliefs. The planet had its own policing force, so it could remain neutral in the galactic arena. Most of society considered it a picture of paradise. A perfect place for families.

This is the world where Thermonte and his crew were landing. This is where their mission was at. Because under that perfect persona of paradise, Serenity had a slight criminal element to it. When the sun went down, the unsavory came out in darkness to play.

They called it the Underground, and it was located in the very heart of the city. The Underground contained many illegal activities some were looking for. Although those who visited kept their political differences at the door, it didn't keep them from getting into trouble here.

One man in particular, Thermonte was sent here to see. He was to collect some money from him that didn't quite make it to the Corlesh Clan. The man's name was Zac Fin. He ran an underground gambling facility in the overnight hours of Serenity, in the capitol city of Damascus.

Thermonte's ship landed in one of the outer docking bays sitting around the city. After a stretch air-car was ordered, Thermonte only took three of his men with him to the gambling facility, Leon Gar and Scotch Kammel. Hester Boyd drove the air-car. He was also the chief pilot of their ship.

It was nearly dark when they set off. When they reached the facility, it had not quite opened yet. Soon Thermonte was sitting across from Zac in his office, and the gambling establishment was preparing to open.

Zac knew why he was there. The collected cut to the Corlesh Clan had been shorted by several thousand credits.

"So what is the problem?" Thermonte asked. Leon stood behind him and Scotch stood just outside the door, making sure they were not disturbed. "Mr. Corlesh wasn't too happy with last months' payment."

"Like I told the carrier, we had a slow month," Zac replied, a little worried about this unexpected visit. "Last month was a slow month for visitors."

"You know, it is regardless of your intake, Mr. Corlesh's cut is one hundred thousand credits per month. It's not a percentage thing." Thermonte explained. "You only sent him half that much."

"I needed the extra to keep this place running."

Thermonte sighed. "This month you owe him two hundred thousand."

"I can't pull that off. We have to pay off the security Locals, so they don't raid the place, and that takes quite a bit." the man said. "I can still swing the one hundred thousand, though."

"I am afraid that won't work."

Thermonte started to think. Perhaps he could start something here that could help him in the future. "Perhaps we could come to some understanding, otherwise, you could be replaced."

Zac Fin seemed to make a strange noise at

that prospect. He knew what 'replacement' meant. "What is your proposal?"

"You put in your one hundred thousand and I will cover the rest. Now if I do you this favor, I may want a favor in the future." Thermonte sat back and watched Zac as he thought about the proposal. Surely he would take it.

"What sort of favor?"

"In time," Thermonte told him. "In time. Don't worry, it will be something that will compliment your talents."

Thermonte looked up at Leon, who just nodded. Leon knew all about his plans, about revenge, and he was all for it. He would rather have his boss in charge instead of that Corlesh boss. He was all behind Thermonte.

After another moment of thought, Zac Fin agreed to the deal. Leon turned and left, heading to the air-car, where Thermonte had left his case. A few minutes later, Leon was back and handed him the case. Thermonte handed the case over to Zac.

"Run this cash through your system and make it look as if it came from this world, and not from the mint. Do you have two hundred thousand already available?"

Zac replied, "It will take time to get it all together."

"How long?"

"Two hours."

Thermonte stood up. "Make it fast. And remember, this deal is between us only. Tell no one about this. Otherwise, Leon here might have to make a private visit."

"Don't worry," Zac replied. "I know that if Mr. Corlesh finds out, I'm a dead man anyway."

As Thermonte and Leon left the room, it was Scotch that asked the question. "So what's the deal?"

It was Leon who answered him back. "We're giving him a couple of hours to get the cash together." Then following Thermonte, he turned and said, "Come on, apparently the drinks are on the house."

Scotch followed. "Sounds good to me."

Two hours later, Thermonte Electrik walked back into Zac Fin's office ready for the payment for two hundred thousand to transport to San Corlesh. Scotch was in the room with them at this point.

Zac handed over the satchel containing the cash. Thermonte took it and looked inside. Then he handed it back to Scotch. "We will count it before we leave, Mr. Fin." he said as he stood up from the seat, reaching out to shake the man's hand. "Very nice to do business with you."

Once they were on board their ship, Thermonte called Leon into his compartment. "Well, what happened?"

"They might know, but it was never mentioned if they knew about your deal with Fin or not." explained Thermonte's friend and bodyguard. "Scotch went out to the car with Boyd for about an hour. Hints perhaps, but nothing definite."

"Keep it up. I want surveillance on them at all times. I just don't trust them as I should. Something is going on."

"I got people all around, boss. The network is building up pretty fast."

Thermonte was thinking all the time about this now. "Would we be able to act now if we need to?"

"Not quite, sir," Leon replied. "The network is becoming big, but we still don't have enough to act against the Clan."

Thermonte just nodded. "Okay then. Just keep me informed on what is going on. You are the most loyal friend I have." he told Leon. "Your loyalty will be well rewarded."

They were in space, heading back to the Ofidian Station with the payment. Thermonte was back in his cabin looking over a few details from some report, not having to do with Serenity. The trip would take them about three days, depending on where the station was located. That information had not yet been transmitted to them yet. It was fifteen hours into the flight when Leon came in to report to his boss.

"What's happened?" Thermonte asked him.

"There was a communication sent ahead to the station by an unknown source, but I bet it was Scotch." Leon told him. "A few hours later, I got word from one of my associates on Serenity, that the Fin Late Night Lounge had been raided and Zac Fin had been shot by Locals there."

Thermonte thought for a moment. "We need to be more careful next time. Make sure everyone knows to stay alert. San Corlesh has to know something is up."

"What if he asked you about it?"

"I won't lie," answered Thermonte. "I will just make it sound as if he was an excellent asset and that it would make it that much easier to deal with Fin in the future, if he trusted me."

Leon nodded. "I gotcha."

"I will get some sleep before we reach Ofidian, but be aware. I think they want to be sure before they try anything."

Leon nodded and walked out. Thermonte

locked the cabin door and went straight to bed.

It took only four months for the ship to be built and delivered. Thermonte, along with his crew and even San Corlesh and several of his posse, walked into the private docking bay to see the new Yacht class ship, gleaming with its newness.

San placed his hand on Thermonte's shoulder. He was standing just behind him. "So, what are you going to call her?"

"My boys and I were talking about it, and we decided on the name of Chimera, a fire breathing creature from the world, one of the outer colony worlds." Thermonte had never seen one, but had read about them in school.

"You ready to take her out for her first run," the godfather said. "Take two weeks off and give her a good run?"

Thermonte looked back at his crew and they followed him on board and within ten minutes, the Chimera lifted off. For his first trip out, he would head to Chotis, to see his mother.

The beautiful ship headed toward the darkness of space, and Thermonte wanted to see his mother. He had gotten word from his friend Derik that she was ill. After the Chimera left the docking bays the Ofidian Station jumped to a new location. Thermonte headed home to Chotis.

CHAPTER SIX
FAMILY AND WAR

Thermonte was home for a time and was spending time with his mother at her home. The illness that had been reported earlier passed quickly and seemed to be nothing for him to worry about. He had come home several times before and as far as she knew; he had graduated from his schooling and had become a salesman for the Ikon shipyards. It gave notability for his wealth and his yacht moored in the spaceport in the city of Necros, where his mother still lived.

He wanted to bring his mother out of the

poor district of Cinder, for he had always loved his mother. He had his friend Derik look in on her from time to time. Thermonte had purchased land east of Necros, which was thickly wooded and was nestled within the misty mountains of Demorn with a beautiful crystal lake at the base of the surrounding mountains. He was building a large home here, with his own personal docking bay within the mountain itself to host his yacht and several other smaller ships.

He had brought her to that location several times, and she was always smiling and was glad that her only son was doing well in life. "You know, I told my friend Edith about you." she told him. "You know Edith, she goes to my church."

Thermonte nodded. "I know her mom. You've introduced us several times." He was smiling. At first he thought she had a touch of dementia, but after a while, it was clear she was just happy to see him. He didn't come around much.

"Anyway," she continued, "Edith has a

niece who is staying with her named Anna, and she will be at church tomorrow and you will meet her at lunch."

"Mother, are you trying to set me up again?" he asked. She had done it to him several times. She wanted him married and to start a family. She wanted grandchildren.

"You're building a home, Thermonte. A wife will give you stability." his mother said.

"Mother," he began.

She pointed her finger up at his face. "You will behave and be polite, won't you?" she said. "She is a nice girl."

Thermonte was smiling. He knew his mother meant well. She was so old-fashioned. "I will behave, mother."

The sermon by the preacher at the Temple of Light was boring, according to Thermonte. Although, he always went with his mother and said all the right things to impress his mother and her friends, he never really heard what the preacher talked about. Instead, he took the time to look around, and he found his mother's friend Edith. Sitting next to her was a young woman that could have been the niece. He didn't see her face, only her long black locks.

After another hour, he was sitting in front of the niece at a local cafe. She was beautiful in Thermonte's eyes and he was in love. His mother had picked well. Soon, they began dating. Thermonte spent most of his time now on Chotis, staying with his mother and watching his home being built. He and his crew still went on jobs that Mr. Corlesh sent his way, and all the time, Thermonte slowly planned his revenge with his crew.

Thermonte continued to spend more time on Chotis, and when missions came up, he would send everyone but Derik on those missions. He would put Leon in charge of the mission. The missions got done, so Thermonte figured everything was going just fine.

Within a year, Thermonte and Anna were

married, and were living in the house he had built within the mountains of Demorn. Several months after, his mother moved in and she was happy that the family was all together again. Thermonte started going on the missions again with his crew using the Chimera, and his private life remained a private life. He never combined work and home. Even though he had an office inside his house that was used specifically for his business.

There seemed, however, to be a problem. Thermonte considered Leon Gar his most trusted employee and friend. It was what Leon was telling him when he got back from their missions.

"I don't trust those three guys." he would tell Thermonte in the privacy of his office. "They are too close to Corlesh."

"How do you mean?"

"They were eating at his dinner at his table every night we were on the station. I never got invited to dinner."

Thermonte looked up at him. He had been

sitting at his giant desk in his office, which sat off to the back side of the home. While he was in there, he was on the job. No one was allowed in there, but for those who worked under him. "Keep your eyes on them, Leon." he told him. "We have another job on Deveron in a week and a half."

"That's Federation territory."

"Yea, I know. Apparently, Mr. Corlesh wants to expand his enterprise." Thermonte had a slight grin. "From what you have been telling, I believe it is a setup. But knowing this, we'll go through with it, carefully."

"Everyone going on this trip?" Leon asked him.

Thermonte nodded. "The usual." he said. "Derik staying here. He does not have the stomach for this. He is good for keeping the women here safe."

Leon agreed. "Shall I contact the others?"

"Where are they?"

Leon huffed. "The station."

"Sure," Thermonte told him. "Follow

protocol and act like nothing is wrong, and contact them. We don't want to alert the Clan we know."

Leon nodded. "Will do, boss." he said and walked out of the office.

The Chimera headed for the border that separated the Republic and the Federation. Thermonte had hired a permanent crew for his yacht, so he and his men could relax before and after missions. Thermonte had a small office in his yacht, where he sat now looking over the plans for the upcoming job. Leon sat in there with him. Everyone else was probably having a drink elsewhere.

The intercom buzzed, and Thermonte instinctively answered it. "Yea, what is it?"

It was the Captain. "Sir, we need to see you up on the bridge now, sir, if you please. We have trouble."

Thermonte looked up and Leon, concerned. This sounded like something new. Both stood up, and Thermonte led the way to the bridge where the Captain was waiting.

"What's the problem?"

The Captain showed him the radar of what was ahead near the border. There seemed to be Federation battleships crossing over and Republic battleships hitting each other hard, fighting it out. "Are you still able to cross the border?"

The Captain nodded. "There are more ships heading this way. Nearly the entire fleet of the Republic at the border. It will be nearly impossible to cross over."

The door into the bridge opened, and Ivan Stromberg peeked his head in. "Hey boss, there is something on the news feed vid-screen you need to see."

They followed him back into the stateroom where the others were watching the news feed on the giant vid screen on the wall. As the newscaster talked, giant words spread across the screen.

BORDER WAR!!

War between the Republic and the Federation officially started just hours ago, when a skirmish took place in the zone known as No Man's-Land, a small territory between the two borders as stated in the Border Agreement; each claiming the other side crossed into their space illegally. The Federation has overtaken the Republic border ships and has since moved on. In charge of the strike on the Federation faction was Admiral Gedor, who made the claim that the Republic struck first. Many have died in the battle, and no one knows who struck first. Stay tuned for more details as they come in from the front.

The Republic and the Federation were at war. How it started, no one knew. All that was known was that many of the Federation warships crossed the border breaking the treaty between the two. And it seemed to Thermonte that they had come too close to it.

"I spoke to Mr. Corlesh, sir." Ivan told Thermonte, and the news feed continued. "The mission has been called off, and he wants us all to report to the Ofidian Station."

Thermonte looked around at him. His eyes met Leon's, who was standing behind Ivan. "Really?" he asked him. "When did this conversation happen?"

"Just before I came and got you, sir." he told Thermonte. "He is the one who put us on to this news feed."

Thermonte glanced over at the Captain who had come in behind Leon. The Captain's head slowly shaking, letting him know that nothing had come through the yacht communications system, and that Ivan was lying.

"Very well." Thermonte said. To the Captain, he said, "Turn the ship around and get us out of here." He left and went back to his office. Leon followed, and the others stayed behind. Thermonte knew it was now time.

CHAPTER SEVEN
TIME TO SETTLE

Thermonte and Leon sat in the office on board the Chimera, discussing what was to come. In all those years of Thermonte sending Leon and the others to do the missions, Leon Gar, on Thermonte's wishes, made other friends, loyal friends, loyal to what Leon called the Electrik Clan.

Leon looked up at his boss and friend. "Is it time?"

"It is us or them." Thermonte replied. "Set it up."

Leon nodded and went to make the call.

Several hours later, the Chimera drifted toward the Ofidian Station as soon as it appeared ahead of them. The officers Thermonte hired had also become a part of the Electrik Clan, and with the help of Leon, Ivan Stromberg, Hester Boyd, and Scotch Kammel all lay dead in the storage bay of the Chimera.

The Chimera docked within the private bay. Once it was locked in and moored, Thermonte and Leon both stood at the opening hatch. When the hatched opened, men were waiting for them, six on either side. These six men were Electrik clan men. As Thermonte led the way out, heading out into the station, he noticed the dead guards laying slumped against the walls of the bay.

Apparently, the Corlesh Clan had been waiting, and knew something was about to happen. A battle incurred. Alarms started blaring throughout the station. Customers and gamblers and those just visiting the station began running wild and abandoning it, trying to get away and stay alive.

"Where are we headed, Boss?" Thermonte heard Leon ask.

"Control room." Thermonte answered. "We need to control the station itself."

"I got that covered, Boss," Leon smiled.

Along with the Corlesh clan defending the station, there were other men from business partners of the Clan helping defend. Thermonte knew no one would bother with a battle on board this station, not with the Border Wars starting. These men were not the only ones fighting the Corlesh Clan.

Besides these six men being friends with Leon, he had made many more friends. Some of his friends were even in the control room. Secretly, they were helping Thermonte and Leon get into the control room with little effort. Many had joined the battle with the six men moving their way to the control room. But with the control room already being under control, Thermonte and Leon moved through the station with ease.

Soon they were in the control room, and which had already been taken over. Now they had to get to the higher level to get into San Corlesh's office.

"Follow me." said one of the control room operators, as he led Thermonte and Leon out a small back doorway, hidden from others. Behind the door, there was a small hallway and a staircase leading up to a small elevator.

"It will get you to Mr. Corlesh's office." the operator said. "There is no one up there to help. Everyone up there works for Corlesh."

Thermonte nodded, and Leon handed him a hand-held bolt pistol. He had one of his own, and they both moved onward toward the elevator. Once inside, they checked their weapons. Thermonte thought his revenge would go differently, but it seemed his own men had betrayed him. They had been dealt with and had been put into a position where he had to move now. His plans were out the window; and what he did now would define him for the rest of his life. He would either make it, or die here.

The door opened, and the corridor was empty. They moved slowly, but steadily, until the end where the corridor turned left. They looked around the corner and saw three guards standing in front of the outer offices. As they watched, Thermonte saw another man walk out of the door. He knew him as Jazy. He knew he had to be taken out. After talking to the three guards, Jazy headed back in the room.

They prepared their bolt pistols and hastened down the corridor with the pistols pointing at the guards. Once the guards noticed them coming, the firing started, and the guards had no chance to respond. They knew they had heard the sounds from within the offices, but Leon was prepared for such an occasion.

The door leading into the offices inside was an old-fashioned manual door. So Leon grabbed the handle and cracked open the door. Thermonte could hear the weapons getting ready to shoot, but Leon tossed in a paralyzer flash grenade. Once the 'pop' sounded, Leon fully opened the door and he and Thermonte entered, their pistols making their mark on the chest of those inside.

The flash only lasted only a moment, but it was long enough. At the last moment, Thermonte saw Jazy heading into San Corlesh's office, and he pulled up his pistol and fired, throwing Jazy forward and the door opened wider.

Thermonte strolled in, his gun pointing directly at San Corlesh. Sitting on the sofa to his right was the man he knew only as Mister Clought, someone he believed to be an associate of the Corlesh Clan. Leon followed, and his pistol was pointed at this Mister Clought.

"Why have you brought this chaos to my home, Monte?" was the only thing San asked, trying to keep some kind of control.

"Don't call me Monte," Thermonte told him quickly. "I have always hated that."

"So why are you here then, Mr. Electrik?"

Thermonte thought for a moment. "Revenge, mostly."

"What have I ever done to you to warrant

this?"

"You gave the order to kill my father." Thermonte said. "He was a deli owner in the city of Strauss in the District of Caste on the world of Chotis."

San Corlesh took in a deep breath. "I have given orders to kill many people, and so I have no memory…"

Thermonte had pulled the trigger, and the forehead of San Corlesh opened up. He was dead.

Mister Clought jerked in fear. Thermonte looked over to him. "Who are you?"

Slightly stuttering, the man said, "I work in the capitol building on Tiere. I inform.." He stopped and looked over at his former boss. Then he continued, "I informed Mr. Corlesh on the comings and goings at the capitol."

"You want to live?" Thermonte simply asked him.

The man nodded that he did.

"Then you now work for me." he told him. "You will keep me informed. But you will see me in my home on Chotis."

With that, he let Mister Clought leave the station with an escort. Then he turned to one of the new friends that had just come into the room, named Bolen. He had been one of the top security leaders on the station. "Get this mess here cleaned up and move the station out of the range of the Republic, somewhere within colony territory. Then I will send Leon back with instructions."

"Yes sir." the man said, walking out to find maintenance. Leon followed Thermonte out from the offices and down the corridor to the elevators. "We're taking the simple way down."

"Where are we going?" Leon asked.

"Back to Chotis first." Thermonte told him, "There is something I need to take care of."

CHAPTER EIGHT
THE GODFATHER

Thermonte sat behind his desk in his office in his home. It had been about a month since he and Leon had returned from the Corlesh killing. The door knocked, and in came his friend Derik Poe. He had just eaten dinner as he always did with Thermonte's family. He was living at the house, because Thermonte had promised him a more prominent position within the new syndicate.

"I think I found something for you, my friend." Thermonte told him. "Leon is heading back to the Ofidian Station, as you know, and he said he could us someone with your skills and learning the entertainment of the station."

Confused, Derik asked, "So what does that mean? Entertainment Director, something like that?"

Thermonte just smiled. "Exactly like that. I want someone I can trust, especially with the money part of it."

Derik thought about it for a moment. "It sounds good by me." he said. "First time off world for me. It's exciting."

"I thought you would like it."

"When do we leave?"

"Leon is heading back there tonight, so you will need to get packed. You're going with him." Thermonte told him and stood up and walked around his desk to stand in front of his childhood friend. "Gonna miss ya around here though."

Derik just grinned gratefully. He held out his hand for a handshake. But Thermonte would have none of that. Instead, he pulled his friend close and gave him a hug; patting him on his back. Derik hugged him back. Nothing else was said, just a couple of nods, and Derik walked out to pack up for his trip.

Soon after Derik left, Leon walked in. "He going?"

Thermonte nodded. "Yeah, you take care of him, okay?"

Leon nodded this time. "I will, no worries." He threw a small packet on the desk as Thermonte was returning to his seat.

Thermonte opened the packet and looked at the papers inside. He sat there quietly looking over each page, reading each work. He had always enjoyed using old-fashioned paper and not one of those computer pads for information.

"Where is he?" he asked Leon.

"At his old place in Cinder. I got men there with him. They beat him pretty bad. But he is alive, for now."

"Okay, as soon as you leave, I will go see him tonight and get it over with on this end."

Khanel's face was covered with blood, dried blood by now. He was sitting in his chair, tied to it like an animal. Four men sat around him laughing and smoking cigars; two of them playing a card game. It was evening and it was dark outside of the building. They all noticed the light from headlights from an air-car, pull up. The four men straightened up just before the door opened and Thermonte walked in, followed by his bodyguard.

Thermonte sat down across from his old boss, Khanel Corlesh, the last of the Corlesh Clan. "Do you know why you are still alive?"

Khanel looked around. He had been in this lifestyle long enough to know what would happen next. He kept his mouth shut.

"I personally killed your father." Thermonte told him. "I just wanted you to know that. What I want to know is, did you turn him?"

Khanel chuckled, then laughed as much as he could. "I treated him well. He kept me informed."

Thermonte stood up, and Khanel expected to die quickly, from a blast to the head. That was not the case. "Wrap it up." he told his men, and the four men each took a container of lithium fuel and doused the building around Khanel. Three feet around, the Corlesh man was untouched. Then the four men followed their boss out the window, but the bodyguard moved in close to Khanel and stabbed him in the gut.

"Just in case." he whispered in his ear and left, throwing a lit cigar on the fuel.

Thermonte Electrik and his men were well away from the building, before the fire consumed it and the fire engineers showed up. Khanel's body was found burned, still tied to the chair.

This crime remains unsolved.

Three weeks later, as the Border Wars continued, Captain Shepherd's battleship came across a bloated, floating body of an individual alone in space. The body of the dead man was never identified.

It was about a year later, after his first child was born; a son named Thoran, Thermonte received a hyper call from Leon, who was running the Ofidian Station. Apparently there was a man there from the House of Taran. He was the biggest crime lord wanting to visit with him in Federation space.

The Ofidian Station was now being operated outside the galactic perimeter of both governments, and within space that was known as colony space. There were no rules or regulations that had to be followed there. So knowing that this man was there to see him made Thermonte nervous.

So under the guise of a business trip, Thermonte and two of his security associates traveled to the station in the Chimera. The trip took about three days.

The man's name was Vik, and he worked strictly with the boss of the Taran Syndicate, Vladimir Taran. In the office that once held the head of the Corlesh Clan, Thermonte sat behind the giant desk staring into the eyes of this man named Vik.

"So, what is it you are doing here, across the border?" Thermonte asked him.

Vik had a thick accent that the Federation was known for, but his words were elegant and almost sweet. "We want to get into this action, of this pleasure space station. It's outside the jurisdiction of our governments and I believe we can bring much more of a cash flow here."

Thermonte thought for a moment. "As I understand the position of the House of Taran, is that you deal in illegal drugs and weapons; which we have no dealing in. Like you said, this is a pleasure station, mostly for gambling. So I do not believe your presence here at this station is good for us. We are not looking to expand in that direction."

Vik laughs, then stands up. He is fiddling with his hands. "That does not seem like a smart decision." he said. "Like you said, we deal in weapons."

"I don't think we are left that

unprotected."

The Federation criminal laughed again. "We have pull within our own naval forces which are willing to help us out when we need help. Can you protect yourself against something like that?"

"Perhaps." The godfather simple replied.

Vik smiled at him. "Perhaps we'll find out." and he left and was escorted from the station.

To Leon, he said, "Move the station around to other colony planetary systems and keep battlements on high alert until further notice. Use fighter scouts before you move."

"Will do, boss." was Leon's answer. Within several more hours, Thermonte was on his way back to Chotis on his yacht.

CHAPTER NINE
THE DEAL

It was about six months later, when it seemed Thermonte had a visitor from somewhere in the outer worlds. One of his security associates, a man named Banko, walked into Thermonte's office with another man that the godfather had once met a long time ago.

Doctor Phaleg walked in behind Banko, smiling his friendly smile at Thermonte. "You've done well for yourself, Mr. Electrik." he said.

Thermonte stood up and returned the handshake Phaleg had offered. Thermonte was smiling. "I've not done so bad."

"You've taken over the Corlesh Clan and restructured it to fit your own needs Well done, my friend." Doctor Phaleg sat across Thermonte at his desk.

"Man has to make a living."

After they were relaxed and drinks had been served, it was Phaleg that started the next conversation. "So it seems you might have some trouble with the House of Taran?"

"Yea, well staying ahead of them for now."

"I can help." Phaleg quickly replied, "and they will not connect it to you. I guarantee it."

"I'm intrigued." Thermonte sat and thought for a moment. What would this cost him, he wondered? "So what do I have to do to repay you?"

Phaleg smiled. "You have to do nothing for me. I just want to start a working relationship with you. Nothing more. I like your style, Mr. Electrik."

"What would this relationship include?"

"No money involved." promised the man. "You need a favor for something like this House of Taran thing, and in return, I may ask you for a favor."

"What is your business?"

"I am planning an exploration trip, so far deep into unknown space, it will take nearly two or three years in an FTL ship to get there."

Thermonte raised his brow. "Sounds interesting. What is an FTL ship?"

"Faster Than Light."

The godfather laughed. "There is no such thing."

Phaleg held up a single finger in hopes to quiet Thermonte's laugh. "Do you remember the first time we met?"

Thermonte remembered.

"I was there ordering the ship to be built for that trip, and now it is ready."

"You mean it goes faster than light?" Thermonte was still skeptical.

"No no, of course not." Phaleg answered. "The ship has been built, but I have a scientist and engineers working on the engines themselves, on a world I call Dragmar."

"Where is the Dragmar?"

"A week outside of the known galaxy in light-speed."

Phaleg had told him a lot, and Thermonte knew this. "So what favors would I do for you?"

"Well, for now, through your business and connections, I could use someone to help recruit for this trip. And I would need people with no families or anything like that. I don't mind the criminal element, but they need to be the best at what they do."

After several minutes, Thermonte thought he might give this a try. "Sounds like an okay deal. Do you have a recruit in mind?"

"So I take it this is a yes, my friend?"

Thermonte extended out hand. Both shook on the deal. "It is a yes. So who do you have in mind first?"

"There is a rising star within the Federation Navy. A man named Gedor. He is a foolish man, but he is the best at what he does." Phaleg just smiled.

"And where is the best place to find this man?"

"I believe he is the threat the House of Taran warned you about. So he may come to you."

As they concluded their visit, and Doctor Phaleg was about to leave, Thermonte asked him a question. "About this exploratory trip you have planned; what is out there? What do you hope to find?"

Doctor Phaleg just smiled that smile. "Water, my friend, and I know it is out there. I just got to get there."

Thermonte and Banko made their way back to their space station. They had gotten word that a small Federation fleet was on its way. The godfather knew it was because of the threat by the House of Taran. The Chimera had just docked in the private bay just moments before the fleet of three Federation battleships arrived. The fleet's guns were all directed at the station, and they were hailing the station for communication.

As he was walking off the Chimera, Thermonte's personal comm buzzed. It was the control room. "They are asking for you, sir."

Thermonte quickly replied. "Ask for an Admiral Gedor. Ask him if he might come on board to discuss the situation and bring him to my office."

"Yes, sir."

About a quarter of an hour later, Admiral Gedor and two of his officers were being escorted to Thermonte's office. Gedor looked to be a proud man. He wasn't very tall, but the way he walked, projected that he was taller than he was. After the first few moments of speaking, Thermonte realized that Gedor thought himself to be someone of great importance.

The first thing out of Gedor's mouth, as he was walking into the office was, "I take nothing off of anyone." He was loud and sounded sure of himself.

"So what makes you think I'm here to take anything off from you?" Thermonte shot back.

That made Gedor angry, and when his men put their hands on their pistols hanging in their holsters, Thermonte's men already had their weapons out and pointing at their heads. The godfather then said, "Maybe we should all just calm down, Admiral."

Gedor thought about it for a moment, then agreed, relaxing himself down slowly. "So what am I doing here, and not out there blowing away this space station?"

"There are too many innocent people on this station, so why would you blow it up?"

Gedor just smiled, and in his arrogance, he said, "It will not intimidate me at all. No one is innocent, and if they are here when I strike, then they go down with the station. I started this war; and no one is the wiser.

Both sides blame each other. So I will easily take down this station with no problem. My men are loyal to me, so no one will care."

Thermonte leaned back in his chair. "So tell me, Admiral, what can we do to not have you destroy this station?"

"The House of Taran wants this station." Gedor told him straight out. "Of course they will share with you. They get seventy. You get thirty."

"I took this station from the Corlesh Clan myself. I get eighty and the House gets twenty."

Gedor smiled. "I don't think so. The House of Taran has many more resources than this little Electrik Syndicate. The House gets control."

Seeing how quick the pride came out in this man, Thermonte thought it was about time to dangle the deal. "How would you like to take control of your own fleet; or should I say your own armada?"

"Are you saying you have an armada hidden somewhere?"

"Let's just say, I have access to one." replied Thermonte. "The job is yours if you want it."

It appealed to Gedor, and Thermonte knew it. "What do I have to do to get my own armada?"

"Nothing."

Then one of Gedor's men heard something in his ear, which held a military grade ear com. He then leaned in and tapped Gedor on the shoulder. "Sir, there are Republic battleships moving toward our sector. We need to get back now, sir."

Frustrated, Gedor stood up. "We'll take this up later, Mr. Electrik. I need to get back."

This told Thermonte that this Admiral Gedor did of those above him he had to listen to. "Tell you what, you fight your war, and when you want to make a deal, just come see me at my home on Chotis. Leon here will see you there with no trouble and no harm will come to you."

"We'll see." was the last thing Thermonte

heard from Gedor as he moved out quickly heading for his shuttle craft.

"Once we leave, get everyone off the station, and move this thing to our hiding place." he told Leon Gar. "Then you guys get back to Chotis. We're shutting this thing down for a short time."

"Will do, boss."

CHAPTER TEN
TWO YEARS LATER

The Border Wars continued for the next year and a half, almost to the day. Before the war ended, it was leaked out that Admiral Gedor had started the war, and evidence was found that he had done so against Federation orders. Who had leaked this information? Thermonte didn't know, but he knew soon, that perhaps Gedor would come and see him, a little less arrogant.

Within that time, Thermonte and his wife had had another child; a daughter named Alexeena. Also, through this time, his mother had become ill. She continued to push for her son to attend her local church, but Thermonte never went anymore. Although, she took Anna, Thoran, and Alexeena to the Demorn Church of Light, located within several miles of their home. It was a mountain church, and not a very large one like the Temples within the cities. But his mom enjoyed it and supported it wholeheartedly. Anna and the children also enjoyed going there with her mother-in-law.

It was one evening before Thermonte's mother made her way into his office where he sat with Leon and Banko just talking about what was next in the business. Once he saw his mother come in, he sent the two men out. He knew something was up, for she had never been in his office.

"So mom, what's wrong?"

She was sauntering around the room, looking at the photos on the wall which most were of his family, and behind his desk were photos of where he has been on his travels, and also galactic maps. So it took a moment before she answered.

"It's you, Thermonte." she finally replied. "You were such a sweet little boy. I don't know what happened to turn you into a harsh man. You don't even come to church anymore, even during the holidays. You are missing out."

"Mom, I don't have time." he said. "My work is important, and it keeps this family together."

"You spend most of your time away from family."

"What I do, keeps the family here. I do everything for the family." Thermonte was getting irritated with his mother. Why was she in here starting this with him now?

"You need to go with the family to church, Thermonte," she said. "That is something you need to do with your family. Taking one day out of your life to do that will go a long way."

"I told you my work is important…"

His mother stopped him right there, before

he said anything else. "You are a criminal, Thermonte. I know what you do, and who your business partners are. They look seedy and most dishonest. You need to turn your life around before it is too late."

It took him back. He didn't know how to respond. All his life he wanted to please his mother, and now it seemed his mother was not pleased. To make things worse, it now seemed his mother had always known what his business was.

But a knock at the door, and Leon sticking his head intended to end this conversation. "He is here, boss."

"Think about what I said." she said, before leaving her son to his criminal activity. "You need to atone, or you could lose everything. Nothing matters, but your walk in the Light."

Then she left, and a few moments later, Leon and Banko followed Gedor into the office. When his mother left, Thermonte sat back down behind his desk and got back to work.

"I need to make that deal." Gedor was

feeling anxious. He had been on the run and hiding for over three weeks now since the war had ended.

"And what deal was that?" Thermonte asked.

"I want to work for this friend you have."

Thermonte thought for a moment. "Maybe I should just turn you in to the Republic; or better yet, perhaps the Federation will pay more."

Gedor moaned.

Thermonte laughed. "It will take about a week to get a transport here to pick you up." To Leon, he said, "Take him to the apartment next to the docking bay, and don't let him out. I don't want to see him until he leaves."

"You got it, boss," replied Leon, grabbing Gedor by his arm, and moved him toward the hidden doorway behind his desk.

Two days later, Thermonte's mother passed on. They held her funeral at the Demorn Church of Light, and it was the only time they saw Thermonte Electrik there. They buried her in a mausoleum he had specially constructed for his family in the Demorn cemetery. He remembered his last talk with her, and now he knew why she was so persistent in his changing his ways. Perhaps, he thought, he could do so in the future.

Although, it would have to be further in the future.

Soon after, things turned for the worst for Thermonte with his family. After his mother's death, which hit him hard, Thermonte seemed to spend more time working and extending his syndicate throughout the Republic. Anna Electrik, along with her children, Thoran and Alexeena, disappeared. Thermonte had found a note telling him she had walked out on him and their marriage.

He sent Leon to go find them, but he came up empty. That was the moment Thermonte Electrik took up drinking heavily.

His son, Thoran, came back into the picture many years later and joined his father in the business; but he would never hear from his wife and daughter again.

CHAPTER ELEVEN
JONAH

Twelve years later.

With his wrists in cuffs and his legs in shackles, Jonah sat in the back of the prison transport heading to Black Star, the Alliance secret dark prison. The facility had been constructed for people like himself, far among hidden stars. Because he had been labeled a terrorist Jonah was not given a trial, or any chance to prove otherwise. Jonah had never considered himself a terrorist. An assassin for hire, perhaps, better fit the description of his line of work. How exactly he got is his current situation, he wasn't sure. One thing he knew for sure, though, was that he had to have been set up.

Jonah was very good at his job of choice; so perfect in fact, that he could have never gotten himself captured on his own. No one in galactic society knew how he looked. The only description that had ever gotten out to the Locals was the color of his eyes. "They were shiny blue, so light that they looked like glass," were the exact words used. For a long time, he had been on the Alliance's most wanted list, classified of course.

His mind switched to just who could have set him up. He had gotten captured on Tiere, the capital world of the Alliance. Simon Kohl, one of his few trusted informants, was on Tiere. He was a short, seedy-looking man who believed himself to be one of the intellectual elite. Jonah could see Simon ratting him out to someone for fear of his own life, but Simon wouldn't set him up alone. However, he was the only lead so far that he had.

Jonah's target had been the Senator of Chotis. He was not a high priority target, so the security for him was minimal. It was going to be an easy job. Thinking about it now, it had been too easy.

He had lined up the sights on the sniper rifle to the head of the Senator making his way out of the Alliance Senatorial Building. There would be plenty of time to get away when the job was finished. Before the Senator disappeared around the corner, he pulled the trigger, and the Senator fell. It had been smooth and quiet. As he began dismantling the rifle, the door of the room he occupied burst open, and the Locals came through the door, guns out of holsters and pointed at him, followed by an Alliance Agent.

The Agent's name was Jon Vega, and Jonas knew him. He knew him because this same Jon Vega had been after him for nearly two years now. Now he seemed to have him. "You finally caught me, Vega. Someone had to have turned me in," he said to him.

Jon Vega stood there and watched as the prisoner was handcuffed. Jon replied, "It doesn't matter; you're not going to be free anymore in this lifetime."

Now he was being transported to Black Star. He placed his right hand inside his left, took his thumb, and started digging hard at his wrist. Soon drops of blood began seeping out. Jonah was not going to be going to this secret prison. Soon a slit formed in his wrist just above the arteries, and he used his thumb to slide out the hidden skeleton key he had stored there many years ago. Quietly he flipped on the key's power and placed it close to the cuffs' computer, and it searched for the cuffs' combination. A few moments later, the cuffs snapped open, and Jonah did the same to the shackles.

The single guard sitting across from him with the rifle had started falling asleep. The shackles had been attached to the flooring of the shuttle but had fallen away, so he quickly jumped at the snoozing guard, his elbow crushing the man's neck. The guard gave an uppercut to him, knocking him back. As Jonah fell, he grabbed the pistol from the guard's side holster and shot the guard in the face before the guard could react again.

The guard fell back against the hull, then slumped over dead.

As Jonah stood up, he heard the announcement over the speaker. "Coming back into real space now. Twenty minutes to Black Star docking. Get the prisoner ready, Case. He is nearly out of our hands."

Jonah smiled to himself. He made his way to the pilot's cockpit and slid open the door. Out of the viewport, Jonah saw Black Star in the distance. The co-pilot looked up, and before he could say anything, Jonah shot him in the neck. The pilot switched on the distress signal, just before he died. Jonah pulled the pilot from his seat and took over. Soon the transport shuttle had turned around and vanished back into hyperspace.

Jon Vega was eating lunch in a corner cafe on

the busy streets of Sandal, the capital city of Tiere. His boss, Commander Dorman, slid into the chair across from him. "Jonah never made it to prison," he stated, trying to get a reaction out of him.

There was no reaction from him at all. He just looked back over his coffee cup. "How far did he get in that shuttle?" Jon had walked Jonah to the shuttle himself and watched it lift off.

"They found the shuttle on the Synoa mining colony, abandoned. Apparently, he took a job on one of the carriers heading toward the seven moons of Gin Kojoda. That is all we know."

"You think he is coming back here?" Jon asked him.

Dorman nodded. "Very possible." He stood back up. "I'd watch your back. He might be after you for catching him."

I don't think so, Jon thought as the Commander walked away. He knew where Jonah might go.

Erik Bond's office was a bit run down, located in a part of the city that was considered shabby, and that was known for its criminal morals. There were, however, many honest people living in this sector of Necros. The rest of the city was thriving as this sector continued to fall into destitution. This was fine for the business Erik Bond was doing.

He ran an employment service of sorts. He found jobs for those who could not get jobs by any other means. Like a hit man.

A man walked in, closed the door, and walked up to Erik, who was sitting behind the desk. "What can I do for you, sir?" Erik asked, smiling.

"Do you know a man named Simon Kohl?"

Erik looked him over. "You a Local?" he asked, referring to the police.

The man shook his head. "No, he was a friend?"

"Then what do you want from me?"

The man sat down in one of the cheap chairs in front of the desk. "You hired him to find someone to kill the Chotis Senator. I want to know if this was your job, or if someone came to you with the job?"

Erik was taken aback. "Are you sure you're not a Local?"

"I'm not a cop," replied the man. "I'm the one who did the job."

After a few moments, Erik let out a sigh of relief. This man was someone in his world. "And you want more money," he finally replied.

"I want to know who gave you the job."

"My clients don't like to be revealed; its what keeps me alive, and in business."

The man pulled out a knife, its blade stained with dried blood. "Simon gave me your name with his dying breath, because he, too, didn't give his clients' names out."

It only took a second for Erik to change his mind. "I only met with a woman, called herself Soshiana. She was stunning, long black hair. She was thin, but strong as a bull." Erik paused and stared at the man, hoping to see some sign of acceptance. There was none.

Erik continued. "She dressed nice, and she came to me, just not here. It was over at Garden Park in the central sector of Necros. She gave me the details there. She never said if she worked for anyone. I assumed it was her job. She paid in cash."

The man just stared at him. "Is that the only name she gave you?"

"Yes," Erik nodded. "And there was something odd about her. No emotion, never even smiled, everything straight up."

The man seemed to think about it. Then he picked up the knife, stood up, and put it away. "Thank you, Mr. Bond. And if you ever have a job, look me up."

Erik stood up, being cordial. "I don't know your name, sir."

"Jonah."

"Just Jonah?"

"Just Jonah," the man confirmed. "Like, just Soshiana."

Jon Vega stood in the office of Simon Kohl. The man's body was slumped against the wall with his head leaning back, and his eyes were open but dead. The Tiere Local Agent, Ben Gettel, stood up from the body and turned toward Jon.

"Looks like a single stab wound in the gut," he told him. "Are we sure this was Jonah?"

Jon looked around, nodding. "Yea, I'm almost certain. It's where the trail led. We need to look around to see if we can find any evidence of where he might have gone next."

Ben began rummaging through the filing cabinets, and Jon sat down behind the desk and looked around. The top of the desk had been cleaned off, although it seemed as if several of the papers had been tossed onto the floor. He picked them up and looked at them. Nothing. Just advertisements and junk mail. He then opened the top desk drawer and found more papers, a bit of cash, and a file folder.

The papers were nothing, just more junk and bills. The folder was another matter. It held jobs he had been given to give to Jonah. The file folder contained all of Jonah's appointments, and there were many.

"I think I found what we need," he said to Ben, who turned around and walked up to the desk. "When we catch him again, we'll have more to charge him with."

"Is all that about Jonah?"

After a moment, Jon found what he was looking for. "Jonah was caught assassinating the Chotis Senator. This job came from a man from Chotis," Jon said. "From one Erik Bond." He turned to Ben. "Who's the Agent on Chotis?"

Ben smiled. "Her name is Saffron Baye."

Jon looked up at him and saw the smile. He used to date Saffron many years ago before he became an Alliance Agent. They were together when he had had Ben's job here on Tiere, as a Local Agent. "When did she get promoted?"

"Four years ago. Ray retired," Ben told him. "She was his second."

Jon let out a sigh. "Well, contact her for me, and tell her to expect me."

The Tiere Agent stood straight up. "It must not have ended well between you two."

"It was a mutual breakup," Jon told him. "Career choices and such." After a few moments, Jon stood up, taking the folder. "Just let her know I'm on my way."

"Sure thing," Ben replied.

Three days later, Jon arrived at the Local Agent office in Angora, the capitol city of Chotis. He saw Saffron sitting behind her desk. Her red hair was no longer down her back but was now cut just above her shoulders, but Jon noticed her bright blue eyes still shone when she smiled.

"Well, well, if it isn't my old beau, Jon

Vega," she said before anything could come out of his mouth. Saffron continued, "Fancy seeing you here after you broke my heart."

Jon closed the door, finally, and walked on inside. "As I remember it, the breakup was mutual."

Saffron smiled. "You broke up with me so you could become an Alliance Agent. Besides, if you hadn't, I probably would be sitting in a cottage somewhere worrying about your health or something."

It finally occurred to him it was a joke. "Ben set this up?"

She nodded and laughed a little. "Yea. He told me he picked on you a bit."

Relieved, Jon sat down across from her. Then she sat up straighter and spoke. "So I hear you tracked the infamous Jonah here."

"Yea, I believe so. I think he came to see a man named Erik Bond, who issued the job for the Chotis Senator assassination."

Saffron handed him a card she had written up for him. "And I found him. He has an office in the city of Necros, north of here. We can be there in a couple of hours."

"The sooner, the better," Jon said. "The last man he visited ended up with a knife wound in the stomach."

Both stood up, and Jon let her lead the way out the door. "I have an aircar waiting outside."

Two and a half hours later Jon and Saffron walked into the office of Erik Bond. Erik was surprised when they showed him their identifications. "What can I do for the Alliance Agent Corp?"

Jon took out the folder he had taken from Simon Kohl's office. He took out the paper about the Chotis Senator and slapped it down on Erik's desk. "You hired Simon Kohl to get someone to kill the Chotis Senator."

Erik was surprised. Beads of sweat started to form on his forehead and neck.

'Oh no," he thought to himself. He glanced at the paper, and he knew they knew. "It was only a job."

"Your job is to hire criminals to kill decent people." Both Saffron's voice and posture showed anger.

Jon tapped her shoulder, trying to calm her down. "So you admit this was your job?" he asked calmly.

Erik just nodded, shamefully. There wasn't much else he could do.

"Now I have another question," he continued. "Has Jonah come to visit you?"

Suddenly, he remembered the knife Jonah had pulled out in front of him. He didn't want to see it again. Erik thought about it for a minute before answering the question. This would be the first time he had ever sold anyone out. He remembered what he told Jonah. It would be the second time.

"He was here," he finally said. "He wanted to know who gave me the job."

"Did you tell him?"

"I told him that a woman calling herself Soshiana found me in Garden Park."

Soshiana worked for a man known

throughout the galaxy as the Godfather of the Galaxy, Thermonte Electrik, and was a name known to Jon. But Soshiana was no ordinary woman. She was a bio-tek, the only one known to exist still. Bio-tek production had been outlawed decades ago. It seemed that the process of combining technology with flesh, even near-death flesh, made those who were operated on to go mad, killing others or themselves.

But this Soshiana was one of a kind. One, she was strictly loyal to Thermonte, and no one else. Two, the problem with the other bio-tek experiments seemed to have been fixed. He had always wondered who had done the job on her.

Jon turned to Saffron. "I know where to go now." He picked up the paper from Erik's desk and placed it back in the folder. "You want to come?" he asked her.

"Wouldn't miss it for the world," she answered, then walked to the door and motioned for the Locals to enter before turning back to Erik. "Erik Bond, you are under arrest for conspiracy in the death of Senator Lawler of Chotis, and anything else we can find."

The Locals took Erik into custody and cuffed his hands behind his back before taking him out the door. "Contact the Agency in Angora, and have him transported to the prison there. I will deal with him when I get back."

"Yes, Ma'am," one of the Locals replied.

Jon looked at her. "Not going to let the Locals take care of it?"

"You have been away from the Local Agency. Death of a senator is Planetary jurisdiction. "

It took two days from when Jonah left Erik's office to find Soshiana. Or, in other words, Soshiana found Jonah. He was in Garden Park when she came up to him.

"You're the man they call Jonah," she just stated.

"And who are you?"

"I'm Soshiana," she replied, holding her hand out for a greeting.

Jonah stood up from the park bench he was sitting on. "You set me up," he said in anger.

"No, I did not. But my employer did. And I am here to take you to him."

"Then let us go," he answered.

Soshiana stood there, arm outstretched, her hand opened. "Please be cordial first, Jonah. Shake my hand."

Jonah just looked at her. This woman was strange. He finally reached out and shook her hand. *DNA scan*, he realized. She smiled and said, "Follow me; it's time to meet my employer."

They took a Skimmer into the mountains just east of Necros. There was a huge house built into the side of a mountain, overlooking a lake. Once they set down, Jonah followed her into the house. The foyer was large, with dark hardwood floors. It was minimalistic and lit very dimly. He saw a painting of an older lady on one of the walls.

She pointed to a closed door on the side. "That is the den. He is in there waiting for you." Then she turned to go further into the house.

"Where are you going?" he asked her.

"I have other things to do," she replied, walking away.

Once she was out of his sight, Jonah reached down from his boot and removed the knife he had used against Simon. He slowly made his way to the door, waiting to be attacked, but no one struck. He opened the door and walked in.

Sitting on the sofa on the far side of the room was a big man, overweight by the looks of him. He had a mustache and neatly trimmed goatee naturally colored to cover up any grey. He had a drink in his hand, and he waved it around as he spoke. "It's about time you showed up, Jonah. I have always wanted to meet the great secret assassin."

Jonah gripped the knife in his fist. "So you

set me up to go to prison," he said harshly.

"I knew you would escape and find me," Thermonte told him. "I had to find out just how good you were."

"What are you talking about?"

The fat man took a drink. "I want to offer you a job, Jonah. You would become so rich, and I can guarantee that the entire galaxy would believe you to be dead. But you would be rich and alive."

Jonah just shook it off. "I'm already rich. I have millions in cash."

"Not anymore, my friend," the Godfather replied. "All of that was seized when they captured you."

"Because you sold me out."

"Ehh," was the reply. "Minor detail. I will replace all that just for you to sign up to work for me." He took another drink.

Jonah didn't say a word. He just thought about it. There was something he needed to know. "So why did you set me up?"

"As I said before, I knew you would

escape. I wanted to see just how good you are, and you are good," Thermonte said to him. "Escaping right before incarceration, that was excellent work."

"So it was a test?"

Thermonte nodded in agreement. "Yea, that is a good way to put it."

"Do you do this to all your employees?"

"Just the outstanding ones." After a moment's pause and a drink large enough to finish the liquid, he asked, "So, are you in?"

"I don't know," was the reply. Jonah was trying his best to think this through.

"Well, you had better hurry and decide." Thermonte stood up and made his way to the wet bar to his right and walked behind it. "The Alliance Agency Corp are on their way here. In fact, they are almost here."

Jonah looked around almost frantically, instinctively. "Are you setting me up again?"

"Of course not. The Locals are looking for you. You're an escaped criminal, and they are following your trail. Simple as that."

Jonah calmed himself down, though he was still holding the knife, waiting for a fight. "How would you fix it, so they think I'm dead, without killing me?"

Thermonte poured himself another drink while explaining. "I have a facility out beyond galactic civilization. Your face would be changed, your fingerprints and your DNA would be hidden. The entire process takes about nine months, and then you would be given a new name and a new outlook on life."

There was a beep, and Thermonte turned on a nearby monitor. "You better hurry and decide. The Locals are about to land."

What choice did he have? Jonah agreed to join, and Thermonte gave Soshiana the go-ahead. She led Jonah from the room, which would be the last time anyone would see him.

Thermonte Electrik finished his second drink, and as he poured himself another, Jon Vega and Saffron Baye were led into the room by one of the Godfather's associates, followed by Locals. "Nice to see you again,

Agent Vega. Welcome to my humble home."

"Not so humble by my standards," Jon replied. "I think you know why we are here."

"Of course," Thermonte replied, walking out from behind the wet bar. "It's about that escaped convict. He was here. And to protect me, my men shot and killed him."

He nodded to one of his men. They went out and brought in a body and laid it on the floor. Jon knelt beside the body and examined it. It looked as if his face had been shot up with a Blast Shot, a projectile weapon. "We sure this is him?" Jon asked. "His face is gone."

Saffron handed him a DNA scanner. Jon took it and touched the face and waited for the result. It came out positive. "It's him," Jon said, still somewhat wary of the result. "It's Jonah."

Then he stood up and looked back at Thermonte. "So you hired him to kill the Chotis Senator, and then killed off the assassin?"

"Now, why would I do that? Senator

Lawler and I were great friends. We appeared together several times at public events."

Saffron grinned. "A criminal and senator together."

"Just because I am rich, doesn't make me a criminal, Agent Baye. And unfounded accusations will get the Agency into trouble," Thermonte said seriously. "Now I would hope you would take this body and leave."

Jon knew he was right. His name was not on any paperwork he had gathered on the Senator's murder, and neither was Soshiana's. Thermonte Electrik's tracks were covered well. They all knew he was a criminal, but without proof, nothing could be done. And everyone here would say it was self-defense.

He ordered the Locals to take the body away. But before he left, he spoke once more to the fat man. "Don't leave anytime soon, Mr. Electrik. We still need to fill out a report for the records."

Thermonte nodded. "Sure thing, Agent."

Twelve hours later, Jonah was led to a secret landing port hidden in the mountains. Soshiana watched him board, and the ship took off for the facility far out beyond civilized space. To the galaxy, Jonah the assassin was dead, and the Godfather of the Galaxy was considered a hero.

ACKNOWLEDGMENTS

First off I would like to give thanks to the Lord Jesus Christ for allowing me to write stories for people to enjoy. I would like to give special thanks to Ed Brookling, for encouraging me to write a story about one of the characters I have created. I would also like to thank my editor, Becky Schulz, for taking the time to read and fix my problems.

Also By The Author:

CONFLICT WITH SHADOWS
INTO SHADOW'S FIRE
THE REDEMPTION OF KINGS
THE MOONS OF MORAG (Kindle Vella)

CHILDREN'S BOOK

CHARLEE KATE MEETS A BINGLEDORF
CHARLEE KATE AND THE CAVES OF VENUS

Published by Strangers and Pilgrims
www.strangerspilgrims.com